JENKIN'S EAR

Also by Dusty Hughes

FUTURISTS *and* COMMITMENTS

JENKIN'S EAR

DUSTY HUGHES

faber and faber
LONDON · BOSTON

First published in 1987 by
Faber and Faber Limited
3 Queen Square London WC1N 3AU

Photoset by Wilmaset Birkenhead Wirral
Printed in Great Britain by
Redwood Burn Ltd Trowbridge Wiltshire
All rights reserved

British Library Cataloguing in Publication Data

Hughes, Dusty
Jenkin's ear.
I. Title
822'.914   PR6058.U34/

ISBN 0–571–14565–5

Library of Congress Cataloging-in-Publication Data

Hughes, Dusty.
Jenkin's ear.

A play.
I. Title.
PR6058.U344D5   1986   822'.914   86–11547

ISBN 0–571–14565–5 (pbk.)

CHARACTERS

BILL JENKIN
RIGOBERTO
FOSTER
BUCHANAN
GRACE SUAREZ
RUIZ
FLEUR
NORA
KATE ZWIMMER

The actress playing NORA should also play the WAITRESS and the DANCER, and the actor playing RUIZ should also play the SECOND INDIAN in the church. The full cast, suitably disguised, must play THE WOMEN OF THE DISAPPEARED at the end.

The play is set in a small Central American country north of Nicaragua. The characters are fictional.

Jenkin's Ear was first performed on 11 June 1987 at the Royal Court.

The cast was as follows:

BILL JENKIN	Robert Urquhart
RIGOBERTO	Alfred Molina
FOSTER	Nickolas Grace
BUCHANAN	John Rowe
GRACE SUAREZ	Clare Higgins
RUIZ	Nadin Sawalha
FLEUR	Harriet Bagnall
NORA	Gloria Roma
KATE ZWIMMER	Phyllida Law
Directed by	David Hayman
Designed by	Geoff Rose

The scenes in the church take place during one long day. All the other scenes are flashbacks moving forward in time from the week before to the morning of the meeting in the church.

ACT ONE

Light grows on BILL JENKIN, *an alert foreign correspondent, in late middle age, frail from recent ill-health. He is wearing a short-sleeved shirt and well-cut drill trousers.*

JENKIN: The middle-aged Englishwoman was standing in the street talking to a group of Indian children. She was wearing a light dress, probably pink, a straw hat, open-toed sandals. Two men crossed the street to join her. The Englishwoman and the two men walked away together. The incident happened in Felicidad. With one of those wretched ironies common in Central America, Felicidad means happiness. Happiness is too big to be a village and yet it isn't quite a town and it's too far out of the city to be called a suburb, because it reaches out into the forested volcanic hills for more than a mile. A *barrio*. A district. A dump. (*Slight pause.*) The incident . . . the two men and the Englishwoman talked for about a minute. One of the men pointed. The other man began to walk back across the street. The Englishwoman and the second man followed him. The woman didn't look worried. Curious perhaps, or concerned. She walked firmly, as they say she always did, with a long stride. The three people disappeared through a gap between two rickety wooden houses. The two men were not armed. The woman did not seem frightened, she looked *tranquilo*. It was an unremarkable occurrence. No one could remember what the men looked like. They were strangers. They were wearing white shirts. Clean white shirts. Nobody noticed anything unusual. (*The light fades on* JENKIN.)

Dappled light, grows slowly. The Church of St Sebastian, Felicidad. RIGOBERTO *is praying. He is somewhere between 35 and 45, difficult to tell, quite un-priest-like, indeed is not wearing his priest's vestments. Then a shaft of light, as if an enormous door opening.* JENKIN's *shadow, the sound of children squabbling in Spanish. After a pause,* RIGOBERTO *raises his head.*

I

RIGOBERTO: (*Casually*) No te moleste, deja la puerta abierta. No hajo nas que rezar.

JENKIN: I'm terribly sorry. I didn't quite catch what you said. (*He has closed the door and moved downstage towards* RIGOBERTO.)

RIGOBERTO: (*With a smile, not turning*) I said, do not bother to close the door, I'm only praying.

JENKIN: Bill Jenkin . . .

RIGOBERTO: The children are very noisy today and sometimes God is a little deaf. Particularly in this country.
(*They are abreast of each other now and* RIGOBERTO *stands and turns to shake hands*.)
I am Father Bravo. Rigoberto.
(*They shake hands*.)

JENKIN: (*Very quietly*) I hope you didn't mind me telephoning you out of the blue.

RIGOBERTO: Not at all. You are very lucky. They cut my telephone off for one year. Now for some reason no doubt sinister it starts to ring again.

JENKIN: (*Again an undertone*) I'm so terribly late.

RIGOBERTO: You don't have to whisper here. This is not St Peter's.

JENKIN: It's very rude of me to be so late.

RIGOBERTO: I'm sure you have a good reason.

JENKIN: The American Ambassador.

RIGOBERTO: Ah . . .

JENKIN: I was kept waiting for four hours.

RIGOBERTO: You come from the mighty to the humble.

JENKIN: I imagine I was kept waiting as a kind of punishment. Though I must say that everything in this country seems to run about four hours late.

RIGOBERTO: The Misquito Indians say that the Dark Gods have captured time and that is why their future is so uncertain. So in Central America in order to cheat the Dark Gods it is necessary to be sometimes a little late. Or sometimes a lot late.

JENKIN: By the same token one could also be a little early.

RIGOBERTO: (*A low chuckle*) Yes. I had not thought. (*Pause*.)

2

But you see sometimes maybe being late will measure the
precise difference between life and death. Being early may
only hasten the event. Did you have good discussions with
the Ambassador?

JENKIN: Free and frank, as they say.

RIGOBERTO: I'm sure many people have the same experience.

JENKIN: Perhaps. By a strange coincidence, the Ambassador
and I are old acquaintances.

(RIGOBERTO *motions* JENKIN *to sit.*)

RIGOBERTO: Do you like a game of tennis?

JENKIN: (*Ruffled*) I'm not really fit enough for tennis these days.

RIGOBERTO: (*Laughs.*) No, not to play now. But you like it.
You watch on television.

JENKIN: Oh, yes, yes I do.

(*Slight pause.*)

RIGOBERTO: Wimbledon is now.

JENKIN: Yes. I think it is. It must have started this week. You
play?

RIGOBERTO: Not here. There are no courts. But in California
when I was at college. (*Performs a convincing left-handed
cross-court passing shot.*) McEnroe.

JENKIN: (*Exhaling*) Ah, yes . . .

RIGOBERTO: I like his personality.

JENKIN: An American.

RIGOBERTO: I am not anti-American. Are you?

JENKIN: Oh no. Some of my best friends. Very best friends.

RIGOBERTO: You have this cricket.

JENKIN: Cricket, oh yes . . .

RIGOBERTO: Slow and *subtil*.

JENKIN: Very peaceful to watch.

RIGOBERTO: Who wants to go to sleep? (*Enthusiastically*) Tennis
is question answer, question answer. Then final resolution.
Tension tension then a little death.

JENKIN: Were you good?

RIGOBERTO: Yes. I had one set from Connors but he was only
14. Still, I was good if you don't mind me not too modest.
(*A pause.*)

JENKIN: I wanted a little about your pastoral work here.

RIGOBERTO: I'm not sure that I can give you what you want. You want from me a good story for your newspaper which although a good newspaper is not a newspaper normally associated with theological matters. For a general readership there will be a coarsening and cheapening of the issues. There will be, I imagine, a great playing up of the conflicts between the Vatican and the priests in Latin America, forgetting the innumerable ways in which we are united. There is an issue of poverty. Of course. You can see it all around you. But we all agree that the Church is more importantly concerned with spiritual salvation. There is no conflict with His Holiness on that, I assure you. Then there is the problem that you are not a Catholic, I don't think, are you?

JENKIN: I apologize, but no.

RIGOBERTO: Your telephone call catch me unprepared.

(*Uncomfortable pause.*)

JENKIN: I quite understand if you don't want to talk to me. I'm glad to have met you, in any case. I've heard a great many good things about your work. It would be a pity to have left without meeting you.

RIGOBERTO: Where are you staying?

JENKIN: The Intercontinental.

(RIGOBERTO *pulls a face.*)

RIGOBERTO: You came by car?

JENKIN: Yes.

(*Pause.*)

RIGOBERTO: It would not be prudent to place reliance on a journalist in my country. Your standards are higher in Europe.

JENKIN: Not a great deal.

RIGOBERTO: I think so. The usual Central American headline is about a woman who gives birth to a chicken. This is the kind of thing that sells newspapers here. It is usually some poor child that has been born terribly deformed. Or the only connection between the woman and the chicken is somewhere in the imagination of the reporter.

JENKIN: There's no reason why you should trust me.

4

(*A pause.* RIGOBERTO *sits.*)

RIGOBERTO: Let me tell you one thing. Yesterday some men
   came to Felicidad to try to kill me. They came here and
   then they came to my house. Fortunately a friend of mine
   was able to warn me. So I was not here when they came.
   After a few hours they became bored and went away again.
   This is the way it happens here.
   (*A pause.* JENKIN *does not react.*)
   Last year I went to the police gaol with a Jesuit, Father
   Ramirez, who was staying with me. We had heard that they
   were torturing two women that they were holding. A man
   stopped us at the door and put a pistol to Rodolfo's temple
   and fired into him with a dum-dum bullet. He was standing
   as close to me as you. I think that they meaned to kill me.
   He was only passing through. It is as casual as that. I am
   still alive. He is dead.

JENKIN: I've seen a lot of death. I've had to watch some very
   nasty wars.

RIGOBERTO: You must be brave to put yourself in danger so
   often.

JENKIN: I'm really a very ordinary sort of coward. Survival is
   often mistaken for bravery. The myths are very persistent.

RIGOBERTO: Recently I have seen slogans painted on the walls
   here. 'Be patriotic. Kill a priest.' That means me of course.
   I do not want to involve you in any danger. There is too
   much waste as it is.

JENKIN: I think I may have reached the age when even the most
   silly kind of exit is less important than other things.

RIGOBERTO: But there is still the problem of trust between us.
   (*The door opens again.* JENKIN *is visibly nervous but*
   RIGOBERTO *is calm.* NORA, *an Indian woman of about 40
   comes on. She walks very slowly.* NORA *kneels, upstage, and
   begins to pray.* RIGOBERTO *walks up to her and says a few
   words to her quietly. She nods.* JENKIN *watches.* RIGOBERTO
   returns.)
   I don't encourage them to kneel. She must. It's right for
   her.

JENKIN: I always thought kneeling was more comfortable?

RIGOBERTO: These people have been on their knees too long.

JENKIN: Weren't you kneeling when I came in?

RIGOBERTO: I will kneel if I am alone with God. (*Pause.*) There is another problem. The problem that you have come here for one thing, but say it is for another. You want to know why Mrs Tennant was killed? And who by? And you don't say this on the telephone or now.

JENKIN: It didn't seem to be a very sensible thing to say on the telephone.

RIGOBERTO: No. Perhaps not.

JENKIN: You know that she's dead?

RIGOBERTO: A friend of mine told me. They said they had found some bloodstained clothes of hers. I didn't know her well, I'm afraid. She was a bit of a . . . busybody. But it is a terrible thing. Terrible.

JENKIN: It's strange that you say you didn't know her well. The person who told me to contact you was under the impression you were friends.

(*A pause.*)

RIGOBERTO: Who was this?

JENKIN: The British Ambassador's daughter.

RIGOBERTO: I have never met the British Ambassador's daughter. When did you meet her?

JENKIN: I met her at a reception the day I arrived.

RIGOBERTO: (*Raising his arms*) I don't know her. (*Pause.*) I have met another correspondent. . . . Foster.

JENKIN: (*Alert*) When did you meet Foster?

RIGOBERTO: Maybe a week ago. He was here asking questions too.

JENKIN: I would appreciate it if you could give me any information you can about Mrs Tennant. She was a close personal friend. If she is dead, it is very important to me to find out why she died.

RIGOBERTO: Yes . . . What kind of car you drive?

JENKIN: A rented one. I don't know what it is. Something Japanese.

RIGOBERTO: We will talk. But first. . . . (*Begins to pray, in Spanish*) Dear God, who has received thy son into the holy

6

kingdom, grant him thy eternal grace and grant that we
may be . . .

*The lights change. An impressionistic jungle. Above it, rising out of
the purplish light in the distance is The Christ of La Felicidad, built
in imitation of a sixteenth-century crucifixion by nineteenth-century
American filibusters. There is a small bench with a backrest and a
small metal plate of the kind that usually gives the presenter's name.*
FOSTER, *a fit-looking English correspondent in his late thirties, in a
safari shirt, is bending over the seat examining a large patch of dried
blood. He picks up a bloodstained shoe, examines it and puts it
quickly away in his bag.* RIGOBERTO, *wearing a straw hat, enters
upstage and stands watching impassively. He is carrying a folder.*
FOSTER *touches the blood with a finger.*

RIGOBERTO: Sangre?

    (FOSTER *starts.*)

    (*Softly, with feeling*) Terroristas. Terroristas.

FOSTER: (*Backing away, trying to keep calm*) La gente que venia
    a encon . . . encontrar . . . no se ha presentar.

RIGOBERTO: (*Correcting him*) Presentado.

FOSTER: Yes. Si . . . no se ha presentado.

RIGOBERTO: (*Tightly*) Norte Americano?

FOSTER: Inglès.

    (RIGOBERTO *relaxes. Smiles enigmatically.*)

    Solo estoy mirando. (*More urgently*) Llamar al policía?

RIGOBERTO: Policía? (*A short, mirthless laugh*)

FOSTER: Yes. Si.

RIGOBERTO: Who were you meeting?

FOSTER: I'm a journalist. This is nothing to do with me.

RIGOBERTO: You said *encontrar*. You meet someone.

FOSTER: I'm meeting a priest called Father Bravo. (*Pause.*) You
    know him?

RIGOBERTO: I know him, yes. (*Looks at* FOSTER.) Perhaps you
    and he were meeting same person?

FOSTER: I don't think so.

RIGOBERTO: (*Looks at the blood.*) Someone is killed maybe. It's
    not unusual . . . heavenly peace. Now, as before. (*A pause.*)
    You know how they explain these disappearances? They are

7

communists so they have gone to Nicaragua. Now when someone dies of natural causes we say they've Gone to Nicaragua. You want Father Bravo?

FOSTER: Yes.

RIGOBERTO: Why don't you go to the church?

FOSTER: That's where we were supposed to meet. But he wasn't there.

RIGOBERTO: You know . . . he's a very bad man.

FOSTER: How do you know?

RIGOBERTO: I am him and that is what I am always being called. (*Pause.*) You want to ask me questions about an Englishwoman who is missing.

FOSTER: The Christian Aid office told me that she'd been delivering powdered milk supplies here, and the only person who would know who was the most needy would be you.

RIGOBERTO: Yes, but she never came, and neither did the supplies. The baby milk was stolen. (*Opens the folder.*) Please forgive me. I am also a poet. I wonder if you would take these poems and read them, and perhaps someone in London would like to translate them. (*He hands the folder to* FOSTER.)

FOSTER: It isn't really my area. Have they been published here?

RIGOBERTO: In Cuba. In an anthology. The one about the man who exports piranhas from Brazil to America. Shall I read it to you in Spanish? What is your Spanish like?

FOSTER: Well, you heard. Not brilliant. Perhaps better if I take them. I hope these aren't your only copies.

RIGOBERTO: No. I have others. You know some people make good profit exporting piranha fish to the States. The story of the poem is that if you have two piranhas they will still be alive when they get to their destination because they chase each other endlessly round the tank. But if you have three they will rip each other to pieces in minutes.

FOSTER: I see.

RIGOBERTO: It is a poem about greed.

FOSTER: Yes.

RIGOBERTO: Are your readers interested in what happens in my country? No, you are all interested in this woman.

FOSTER: There was a documentary about her life on television recently.
(RIGOBERTO *shrugs*.) We don't have many heroines nowadays. The popular papers call her The Sister of Mercy. (*Pause*.)
So when did you see her last?

RIGOBERTO: Three months ago. It was the only time we met and at the time I thought it was one time too many. She would not listen. Sometimes I think we have too many Sisters of Mercy here.

FOSTER: Is there anybody else who might have seen her?

RIGOBERTO: Nobody has seen her if I have not.

FOSTER: I'll talk to people in the village.

RIGOBERTO: You could go to the bar. Downhill from the church.

FOSTER: Will you direct me there?

RIGOBERTO: Certainly.
(FOSTER *examines the ground near the seat*.)
It is a tragedy if this woman has been killed. She wanted to do her best for people here. We rely on those kind of people even if sometimes they do not understand our ways.
(FOSTER *opens the folder*.)

FOSTER: Perhaps you can tell me this. There are two nuns who live nearby. I believe that they may have seen something of Mrs Tennant. Can you direct me to their house?

RIGOBERTO: I can, but you won't find them.

FOSTER: They're away?

RIGOBERTO: Gone to Nicaragua.

FOSTER: Nicaragua. I see. You mean they're dead.

RIGOBERTO: No. They are opening a mission there. Let me read you something. I will translate. (*Takes back the folder*.) This I like. (*Reads*) 'My God is the God of justice.'

FOSTER: Listen I really would like to hear you read sometime but I'm on a very tight schedule. I think I'd better go to the bar and talk to people there . . . Would you direct me?
(NORA *comes on. She is carrying a sack. Inside, something round, like a football*.)

RIGOBERTO: Are you with the Norte Americanos, or the naughty Russians, Mr Foster?

9

FOSTER: Sorry?

RIGOBERTO: (*Taken aback*) It was a play on words. Norte, naughty.

FOSTER: Oh, yes . . .

RIGOBERTO: (*To* NORA) Buenas días, Nora.

NORA: Tomas es muerte.

RIGOBERTO: No es muerte.

NORA: Muerte. Muerte.

FOSTER: Who? Who is dead?

RIGOBERTO: Her son. Tomas.

NORA: Muerte. Todos mis muchachos. Miguel. Noel. Ahora Tomas.

RIGOBERTO: Cuando, Nora? Cuando?
      (NORA *holds up the sack, then sinks to her knees.*)

FOSTER: (*Realizing what's in the sack*) Jesus Christ.
      (RIGOBERTO *comforts her. And says a quiet prayer, quickly.*)
      Who did it?

RIGOBERTO: (*In Spanish*) Who?

NORA: (*In Spanish*) The army. They took him away last night.

RIGOBERTO: She said it was the army . . .

FOSTER: Yes, I got that.

RIGOBERTO: They came for him last night. They've killed three of her boys now. Because they are all active in organizing the *campesinos*.

FOSTER: Who is she?

RIGOBERTO: Her name is Nora. She teaches the little ones. She is a member of the teachers' union here.

NORA: (*In Spanish*) Bastards. Sons of bitches.

RIGOBERTO: (*Touching her gently*) Now you will have something to write about. (*Stands. In Spanish*) Come on. You know where we must go.

NORA: No. No. No.

RIGOBERTO: (*In Spanish*) Have courage and trust in God. Trust him. (RIGOBERTO *touches* NORA, *moves off.*)

FOSTER: Where are you going?

RIGOBERTO: To the police. We have to do this. If we don't they will think they can do anything. (*In Spanish*) Trust in God.
      (NORA *stands.*)

(*In Spanish*) Go on. I will go with you. (*To* FOSTER) We were quiet. And now . . . Next week is the happiest day of the year. The feast of St Sebastian when the Indians and the Catholics come together in a procession. It is a celebration of life. (*Laughs bitterly*.) You want to go down the hill from the church. Then turn left into the street and walk for a hundred yards. You will see the bar. It is the only one. Be careful who you speak to. Not everyone will tell you the truth and people who ask questions are not always welcome. I'm sorry to not be help. *Adios.* I hope you find what you're looking for. (RIGOBERTO *and* NORA *go.* FOSTER *is left alone. The lights dim.*)

The sound of a three-piece singing group, two guitars and a marimba. The garden of the British Embassy. A party, evening. A hammock, cane chairs. Sound dips to become background music.
BUCHANAN, *the British Ambassador, is holding court with*
FOSTER, GRACE SUAREZ, *a strong-willed, relaxed woman, and his daughter* FLEUR, *spikily intelligent and nervy.*
BUCHANAN: It seems to be going very well, don't you think? Are you having a good time?
FOSTER: I am, yes.
BUCHANAN: I don't know how much time you're going to spend here, Mr Foster, but you must take the trip down the Patuca river. It's four or five days but you'll find it very rewarding. I'd personally rather spend a week in the rain forest where there's such an abundance of life than visit a lot of old Mayan ruins which frankly all look alike to me. Have you been to the Celaque?
FOSTER: No, I haven't had the time yet. Where is it?
BUCHANAN: North. There's a volcano you can climb and look right down into the bowels of the earth. In the days before democracy one of the generals used to drop his political opponents into it from a helicopter. More interestingly there's quite a rare breed of parakeet that lives inside the cone. There was a brisk trade with the zoos all over the world for a while but the birds simply pegged out after a few days. Eventually it was discovered that they were all

completely hooked on the sulphur. I'm sure there's a moral there somewhere.

(FLEUR *sniggers, catches a sharp glance from* BUCHANAN.)

GRACE: (*Flippant*) The parrots are obviously the souls of dead revolutionaries.

BUCHANAN: Oh, yes, very good . . .

FOSTER: (*To* BUCHANAN) I don't suppose there's very much to do here, is there? For you, I mean.

(RUIZ *enters behind, stands quietly at the back. A politician in his early forties. Well dressed, dangerous looking.*)

BUCHANAN: Nothing much apart from the endless solidarity committees from polytechnics in Salford crawling about the place looking for guerrillas to support and death squads. They think it's all one big cigar advertisement with sexy girls and characters in camouflage shirts. Only they never venture beyond the city boundaries so they only meet the same old loud mouths who are queueing up to tell the same old stories to any fool who will listen. Then they lose their passports and expect us to bail them out.

(RUIZ *steps forward from the shadows.* FLEUR *is shaken by his sudden appearance.*)

RUIZ: There are no death squads here, Señor Buchanan.

BUCHANAN: Of course not, Señor Ruiz. I was saying how difficult it is to convince our left-wing compatriots of this.

RUIZ: I'm sorry.

(*He has turned to* FLEUR *and is staring at her.*)

I must have not heard correct.

BUCHANAN: (*To* FOSTER) Señor Ruiz is a businessman who is doing more than most to help the economy.

RUIZ: We are trying hard.

BUCHANAN: Señor Ruiz helps to sell the artefacts the Indians make. Beautiful things.

(RUIZ *smiles.*)

This is Sebastian Foster, from *The Times*. He's writing a book.

RUIZ: (*To* FOSTER) Oh, yes.

BUCHANAN: Dr Suarez . . .

RUIZ: (*Casually*) I have seen you.

BUCHANAN: And my . . .

RUIZ: (*More pointedly, fixing on* FLEUR) Yes, I know.

BUCHANAN: Where is your wife? Is she here tonight?

RUIZ: I have locked her in the car. She is hysterical. (*To* FOSTER) You won't tell lies about my country, Mr Foster, will you?

FOSTER: Why should I? It's easier to tell the truth.

BUCHANAN: It's a very beautiful country.

FOSTER: I'm not writing a travel book.

RUIZ: What does the truth look like when it has flown halfway round the world? Hmmm? Tired. Yes?

FOSTER: Señor Ruiz, I wouldn't be writing a book if I thought your country . . . the whole of Central America wasn't important.

(RUIZ *allows himself a slight untrusting smile.*)

GRACE: I don't see why. You might be doing it to make money. Or because you were bored.

FOSTER: What are you a doctor of? Exactly?

GRACE: I am exactly a doctor of medicine. In the world I'm a paediatrician, here I'm a sawbones. I cure enteritis, treat rabies, remove bullets, issue death certificates and drink too much in the Intercontinental hotel.

RUIZ: We're so grateful to you, doctor. What would we do without people like you to teach us how to be healthy.

GRACE: Listen. I've just landed up here, I'm not here on a mission.

BUCHANAN: Please, please.

GRACE: (*To* RUIZ) You have very nice eyes.

RUIZ: I'm sorry, I misunderstand.

BUCHANAN: I admire the work you do, Mrs Suarez.

RUIZ: Perhaps I can buy you a meal sometime.

GRACE: Thank you.

RUIZ: Why is everybody so miserable? (*To* FLEUR) Why are you so quiet?

(FLEUR *looks at the floor.* RUIZ *still hovers near her.*)

BUCHANAN: (*To* GRACE) People here can see that you can change things by effort and goodwill. And if you can do it, so can they. Please remember I like these people. I've been here for seven years. I want them to succeed.

13

(RUIZ *bows ironically to* BUCHANAN.)

FLEUR: The music's stopped.

FOSTER: I was in Felicidad yesterday and the local priest told me that one local woman had lost all her three sons because of their political activity. Disappeared.

RUIZ: The priest in Felicidad is a liar and a communist. What were you doing in Felicidad? There is nothing to see there.

FOSTER: Well, as it turned out there was.

RUIZ: These people like to put blame for their own weakness on the backs of the strong. You don't want to get mixed up with such people. They only make propaganda. It might be dangerous for you.

FLEUR: It's cold. I'm going inside.

RUIZ: Is it cold? I don't think so. Stay with us!

FLEUR: Excuse me . . .

(*She avoids him, goes.* RUIZ *remains composed. The music starts again.*)

RUIZ: Señor Buchanan, I have never been to your house before. It is very interesting to me. Can I ask you who recommend this group?

BUCHANAN: My guests?

RUIZ: The entertainment.

BUCHANAN: I'm sorry? Oh, you mean the singers.

RUIZ: So call. And the woman who is to dance.

BUCHANAN: The British Council, I think. I was told we were getting the best. Isn't that right?

RUIZ: You don't hear what they sing about?

BUCHANAN: I'm sorry. I haven't been listening very carefully. I'm going in there in a minute.

(JENKIN *appears at the back.*)

FOSTER: The last song was about a bird.

(RUIZ *makes a small, helpless gesture.*)

JENKIN: I had an extraordinary dream in my hotel. I dreamed I was being made Queen of Tonga. Only I wasn't fat enough so they made me eat thousands of liquorice allsorts. It was heaven.

BUCHANAN: Mr Jenkin, I'm so sorry to have pressed an invitation on you so soon, but we don't get many

14

distinguished people dropping in on us. You must be
terribly jet-lagged.

JENKIN: No. I don't suffer from jet-lag.

(*He sees* FOSTER. *Waves his hands Al Jolson fashion.*)

FOSTER: God! Christ! What are you doing here?

JENKIN: I'm on holiday, dear heart. (*Conspiratorially*) I'm told
we should watch the cabaret. It's about to begin.

(FOSTER *laughs,* JENKIN *mops his brow, pats* FOSTER *on the
arm. The music has finished to applause.* RUIZ *walks off. The
others draw back. Sound of bells and hollow pipes. An Indian
woman enters, dances, briefly. She finishes.* FOSTER *and*
JENKIN *alone.* FOSTER *grips* JENKIN's *hand warmly, smiling
and shaking his head in disbelief.*)

FOSTER: What are you *doing* here?

JENKIN: I'm on holiday.

FOSTER: You're lying. Whenever you arrive somewhere there's
usually a full-scale war within hours.

JENKIN: A myth. You should never believe what you hear in the
papers.

(*The younger man watches the older as he gets into the
hammock, cradling a rum punch.*)

FOSTER: I thought you'd . . . retired from active duty.

JENKIN: Absolutely. I'm practically bionic after the last
operation.

(FOSTER *looks at him sympathetically.*)

Without any of the superpowers that might suggest.

FOSTER: I'm sorry we lost touch. You were very kind to me.

JENKIN: Couldn't work for that bastard any more.

FOSTER: We lost something when you left. Soul . . .

JENKIN: I don't know, I'm not sure. The world's changed. I'm
a bit of a dinosaur.

(FOSTER *doesn't know how to take this.*)

Sorry to hear about you and Jean.

FOSTER: Yes, I don't know what went wrong there. I was never
around much. (*Pause.*) You can't possibly be here on
holiday. It's the end of the world.

JENKIN: I'm looking up an old friend. Someone I haven't seen
for years.

15

(FOSTER *still standing. The music starts again.*)

FOSTER: I know I keep banging on about this but I can't tell you how much you taught me. I was very green.

JENKIN: Rubbish. You always wrote brilliantly as far as I remember.

FOSTER: We all set our standards by you. I felt your presence very strongly when I was in the South Atlantic.

JENKIN: (*Uncomfortable*) Your dispatches were very strong. I thought you did a very good job for them.

FOSTER: I always imagined you looking over my shoulder.

JENKIN: And puking down your shirt. (*Pause.*) Oh yes, I heard a lot of stories about you, jumping in and out of helicopters leaving the other buggers behind. And you're a hero too. Isn't that what I heard?

FOSTER: Oh, bloody hell, no . . . not at all.

JENKIN: That's what I heard.

FOSTER: I kicked a grenade out of the way. It was a reflex action.

JENKIN: (*A chuckle*) It's not the sort of reflex action I've observed amongst war reporters. It's usually throw yourself flat and pray to God it blows some other bugger's head off. What else did I hear? The stories that came out.
(*Pause.*)

FOSTER: Who is it you've come to see here?

JENKIN: A woman called Tennant. One of those absolutely terrifying species of middle-aged English womanhood who scream around the globe doing good works everywhere. I'm rather fond of her. She invited me to come out. I was bored . . .
(*Pause.* FOSTER *sits.* JENKIN *looks at him carefully.*)
Know her?

FOSTER: Vaguely, yes.

JENKIN: We met a long time ago, in Africa. When in the same part of the world . . . sometimes we meet and sometimes we don't, but we have a little ritual. It's very silly really.
(*He reaches in his jacket pocket and pulls out an object.*)

FOSTER: What is it?

JENKIN: It's a tarantula. Made of brass. It sounds very juvenile. I slipped it in her bed once. Now it gets passed between us.

16

From bed to bed. Over the years, using whoever we can persuade to do the dirty deed. Hotel porters, dinner party guests . . .

FOSTER: What's the significance?

JENKIN: Nothing at all. It just says hello.

(FOSTER *smiles, shakes his head.*)

I know what I heard about you. In the Falklands . . . I couldn't understand why you were the only correspondent I ever read. You were everywhere.

FOSTER: Pooled dispatches. The curse of the censored classes.

JENKIN: I heard you'd discovered a new trick. You volunteered to deliver another hack's copy to the censor and then conveniently left it in your back pocket.

FOSTER: I'm sure that was someone else.

JENKIN: I thought it was rather funny.

FOSTER: (*Becoming more and more enthusiastic as he goes on*) I've had a strange feeling about this part of the world for a long time. That the conflict . . . when it comes is going to be massive and bloody, like Vietnam. Remember we used to use that word Vietnamization. You can begin to see it here; the whores, the clip joints, American sailors lurching about smashed out of their skulls; it's tragic. I'm sure the Yanks are going to provoke a conflict with Nicaragua soon. Did you see Ruiz? I couldn't believe it when he walked in here. I've got a hell of a lot of circumstantial evidence that he's behind most of the political killings here. I just want one good piece of concrete proof. One case.

JENKIN: I don't see the connection.

FOSTER: It's all connected. The Americans are covering up for Ruiz. I want the book to move from the particular . . . say one disappearance, to the general . . . the atmosphere of tension, and all the political horse-trading that's going on here . . . I'm almost writing it on my feet. I really do believe this could blow up at any time and it would be a massive *coup* to be in there with something when the whole of Central America catches fire.

(*Pause.* FLEUR *comes on, followed at a distance by* RUIZ. JENKIN *flips the spider.*)

Did you find that in your hotel when you arrived?

FLEUR: (*Keyed up*) Can I join you? Too much yap yap yap.

(JENKIN *slips off the hammock. Makes a drink gesture to* FOSTER. FLEUR *realizes that* JENKIN *has misread the situation and wants to leave her alone with* RUIZ.)

Are you leaving me?

JENKIN: Excuse us. We're only talking shop.

FLEUR: I wanted to meet you.

JENKIN: I'll be back.

(*He smiles. Goes.* FOSTER *follows him.* RUIZ *is holding out two plane tickets.* FLEUR *sees him and turns her back.*)

FLEUR: No.

RUIZ: We are going to Miami.

FLEUR: No, Raul, I don't want to go to Miami with you.

RUIZ: The plane will leave in three hour. The best hotel.

FLEUR: No. *Absolutamente. No!*

RUIZ: When we are in Miami you will be happier. (*Smiles sweetly.*) We will go to Disney World.

FLEUR: I'm going to scream if you don't leave me alone.

RUIZ: I will make love to you all night.

(FLEUR *sits, anguished.*)

FLEUR: Leave me alone.

RUIZ: It is tempting? A little?

FLEUR: I'm staying here. I'm not leaving the Embassy.

RUIZ: You know what I have said. You are not untouchable even when your father is who he is. I don't like these reporters being . . . you talk to no one.

FLEUR: Why was I attracted to you? It doesn't make any sense.

RUIZ: You are in love with death.

FLEUR: (*Shivers*) I hate you.

RUIZ: You want to flirt a little more. Come on, it's a dance.

(*He does a little dance.* FLEUR *goes over to him. He kisses her. She curls her body round him.*)

Come on. You want some coca.

(*She tries to push him off.*)

FLEUR: No. I'm going inside.

(*Music starts up again.* BUCHANAN *comes on, sees.*)

BUCHANAN: Señor Ruiz, your wife is making a scene. She's

18

smashing all the windows of your car.

RUIZ: (*Shrugs.*) Call the police if you want. Or will I?

BUCHANAN: We ought to do something.

RUIZ: You know these singers. They are communists.

(RUIZ *goes.* BUCHANAN *observes* FLEUR *coldly.*)

BUCHANAN: What is going on?

FLEUR: I was dancing.

BUCHANAN: Behave yourself.

FLEUR: Fuck off! I wish I'd never let you talk me into coming here.

BUCHANAN: You realize what a horrible mess there would be if you got into any trouble?

FLEUR: I realize it might jeopardize your career, if that's what you mean.

BUCHANAN: I wouldn't like to push you back into the real world. You're not ready for it. But if I have to I will.

FLEUR: I don't enjoy living here with you both watching me all the time. Mother looks at my eyes every morning at breakfast. She tries to make it look like a kind, searching look, but she's only looking to see if my pupils are dilated.

BUCHANAN: But you do want to be free of it.

(FLEUR *looks down.*)

It would be easier for me to send you back to London and keep paying the bills at the clinic. I haven't chosen the easy way. It's because I love you.

FLEUR: Bullshit!

BUCHANAN: You realize how much that hurts?

FLEUR: That's all you have to say, is it?

BUCHANAN: That's all.

FLEUR: I want to live. I promise you.

BUCHANAN: There's a small paper packet with some white powder in it in your room.

FLEUR: Keep out of my room!

BUCHANAN: You're lying all the time.

FLEUR: It isn't smack. It's coke.

BUCHANAN: Where do you get it from?

FLEUR: Do you think the brave correspondents know you're a spook?

(*A pause.*)

BUCHANAN: All diplomats are spies. We pass on information. Where did you get it from?

FLEUR: You'd do anything the Americans told you to do, wouldn't you?

BUCHANAN: Certainly not. We simply don't have a lot of interests here. Please don't be foolish about my job. I thought we trusted each other.

FLEUR: This place disgusts me and the blandness with which you pretend nothing is happening. Because the Americans want it that way.

BUCHANAN: This is not relevant to what we are talking about.

(JENKIN *and* FOSTER *come on.*)

JENKIN: The Christian Aid office said they were a bit worried. They haven't seen her for a week.

FOSTER: Mr Buchanan, I think you'd better come rather quickly. There's a young woman near the path. Her throat's been cut.

(FLEUR, *who has wandered upstage, lets out an angry, shocked cry.*)

BUCHANAN: This is the absolute . . . *fucking* limit. Here! Show me.

(JENKIN *goes over to* FLEUR, *puts an arm round her.*)

FOSTER: It's the girl who was dancing a few minutes ago. You can see. Just there. I think we'd better try and handle this quietly or there'll be panic.

(FLEUR *is sobbing.*)

BUCHANAN: I can't see very well. She's still warm. Try and be calm. I don't want your mother to come out. (*To* FOSTER) Can you find the doctor woman?

(FOSTER *going.*)

And get the music playing.

FLEUR: The show must go on.

BUCHANAN: Don't be hysterical, please.

FLEUR: (*To* JENKIN, *through tears*) I went to a party in a restaurant by a lake. Somebody saw a body floating in the water in the moonlight. They fished it out. Nobody came to take it away. The body lay there in a heap at the side of the dance floor and everybody . . . carried on dancing.

JENKIN: I'll slip inside and get you a strong drink.

FLEUR: No! Stay here.

(RUIZ *comes on.*)

RUIZ: (*Loudly, melodramatically*) Now what's this I hear about a body? Where is this?

BUCHANAN: There's a young woman over there by the path. Her throat's been cut.

RUIZ: Who is it, do you know? This is terrible. It's terrible!

BUCHANAN: An Indian girl.

(RUIZ *goes off.* BUCHANAN *follows. The music starts up again, loud and jaunty.*)

FLEUR: Thank you. I'm sorry.

JENKIN: That's quite all right.

(FOSTER *and* GRACE *come on.*)

FOSTER: She's over here.

(RUIZ *comes on dragging the limp girl. Followed by* BUCHANAN.)

BUCHANAN: You cannot give orders in my house.

GRACE: What are you doing? Don't move the body.

RUIZ: There is no light.

(FLEUR *is catatonic as the body is dumped.*)

That's better. (*Gestures to* GRACE *to go over.*) Now . . .

(GRACE *bends over the body.*)

GRACE: Will you please get out of my light.

RUIZ: What a place to choose, eh?

(GRACE'*s back straightens. She looks at* RUIZ, *who smiles. She puts a finger to her lips, laughs, walks away shaking her head.*)

GRACE: Oh, hell . . .

(*The woman suddenly rolls over and jumps up, grinning broadly. Does a small bow and backs a way off.* RUIZ *claps and enjoys his own joke hugely. He is the only one.* FOSTER *is transfixed.* BUCHANAN *walks off coldly.*)

RUIZ: You see. Nothing is what it seems to be.

FOSTER: You had me fooled.

RUIZ: They will do anything for money. Even communists.

(*Makes to go.*) People exaggerate our violence of course, but, *mis estimados periodistas*, if you are moving about, let the Ministry of the Interior know where you are going. I can advise you if it is safe or not.

JENKIN: Do you think so?

RUIZ: Of course. I am deputy Minister of the Interior!

(RUIZ *bows, goes. The lights fade.*)

Dappled light again. The church. Door open, noise of children playing. NORA *kneeling.* RIGOBERTO *crosses himself.*

RIGOBERTO: In nomine patris et filii et spirtus sancti.

(JENKIN *stands still for a moment, head bowed but watching* RIGOBERTO. *After a second or two* NORA *gets up and leaves the church.*)

(*Turns to* JENKIN.) I am not sure that I can completely satisfy your lust for knowledge. I am typical of a lot of priests in Latin America.

JENKIN: I realize your situation is very delicate.

RIGOBERTO: Which foot are you kicking with? Is that what you say?

JENKIN: I'm an atheist.

RIGOBERTO: Your account of our struggles would at least be objective.

JENKIN: Objectivity is another name for moral cowardice.

RIGOBERTO: I thought journalists are proud of objectivity. What do you have to replace?

JENKIN: I write what I feel. For what it's worth, which probably isn't very much. 'This is a scandal.' 'This man is a bastard.' I've lost a job or two over the years.

RIGOBERTO: But I can tell you have had a successful life. When one job has gone another good one has followed it.

JENKIN: Oh yes, I've been around a long time. I'm part of the furniture. Like some old commode that's long ago given up its real function.

RIGOBERTO: You are a foreign correspondent on your paper?

JENKIN: I was one for many years. Unfortunately about five years ago, when I was in India, I was in a little argument between a light aeroplane and a tree. I had to be completely redesigned. My insides are like some mad futuristic sculpture.

RIGOBERTO: You are here working . . .

JENKIN: For the last few years I have been given the luxury of a newspaper column to say what I like about anything I like. This has not been the worst fate known to man. I quite enjoy it. I have a licence to be as rude as I like.

RIGOBERTO: But life has been better.

JENKIN: I have an enormous and delightful family. And there's a great deal to be rude about.

RIGOBERTO: I have only met two intelligent Englishmen who cared about what was happening in the world and neither of them understood how people like us could look at your country with envy. Is it a disease you have?

JENKIN: Not at all. To begin with I am Welsh. Although that isn't completely relevant. I have every good reason to like and even occasionally love my country. I've spent a great deal of time away from it.

(*A pause.* RIGOBERTO *sits beside* JENKIN. *Looks at his watch.*)

RIGOBERTO: So I must be clear. You and I, we're not worrying about death?

JENKIN: I'm thinking about it surprisingly little at the moment.

RIGOBERTO: There is no time to worry about death though of course it is always the most important. I only ask God why so many stupid deaths. We call them 'killed deaths', absurd deaths. Because of hunger. Because of having no way of support. Because of injustice and violent greed. There are stupid tragedies all around.

JENKIN: I suppose it's a hopeful sign that however many mangled bodies one sees in a lifetime one never gets used to it. (*A pause.*) I was told that Mrs Tennant was working in Felicidad when she disappeared.

RIGOBERTO: Oh, she was probably here once in a while. (*Pause.*) Would you like a beer?

JENKIN: That sounds like an excellent idea.

RIGOBERTO: Good. There's a bar along the street. I would like to have some small talk. How long have you been in my country?

JENKIN: A week. Nearly a week. (*A pause.*) A beer then.

23

(RIGOBERTO *crosses himself quickly. Turns to* JENKIN.)

RIGOBERTO: A Budweiser. Did you bring your car right up the hill?

JENKIN: No. I didn't think it would make it. It's down below.
(*The lights change.* RIGOBERTO *leaves.*)

The DANCER *comes into a spot. The jungle encroaches everywhere. The* DANCER *has the mask she wore for the dance. It has European features, pink skin, rosy cheeks, a pencil moustache and a goatee. She takes it off.*

DANCER: The Spanish *conquistadores* took everything from the Indians: our industry, our farming, our fishing. We were humiliated over three hundred years. So we put our trust in the afterlife the Catholics promised. Because we never gained anything from other men. We put our trust in the miracles of the saints. History tells us we were not strong enough to survive. But all the time we mocked the *conquistadores* with our theatre. We laughed at the customs. We laughed at their morals. Now we are laughing at the new *conquistadores* too. Our culture will not survive. But the laughter will be heard for ever.
(*She puts on a grotesque mask. An American. Music of a cabaret band, Tijuana style, 'The Shadow of Your Smile'. The open-air restaurant. 'El Rancho', its name hung up among the lights in the trees.* FOSTER *and* GRACE *are sitting at a table. They have finished their meal. There's an atmosphere of intimacy, but brittle and defensive.*)

GRACE: I bummed around Europe with a maple leaf on my rucksack like a million other comfortably off Canuck kids . . . graduated from medical school, got bored as a paediatrician in Toronto. Came here. There's nothing remotely interesting in my background. Unless you count my uncle Cal, who I'm supposed to resemble.

FOSTER: What was he like?

GRACE: He lived in a beach hut near Vancouver and drank himself to death. The last time I saw him he was sipping aftershave out of one of his shoes and listening to Monteverdi. He was an intellectual.

FOSTER: Why did you stay here?

24

GRACE: I came here as a volunteer medical worker. I fell in love
with a helicopter pilot. He turned out to be a womanizer. I
had to leave him. By the time I'd been here for a year, I'd
already fallen in love with the people, particularly the kids.
It's hard not to. There are casualties like me all over Latin
America. Why don't you ever say anything about yourself?

FOSTER: I'm saving it for my autobiography, when I'm old.

(GRACE *not impressed*.)

I don't know, there's nothing very interesting to say. There
is so much going on around me, I'm trying to take it all in.

GRACE: Why do you have to try?

FOSTER: I don't know.

GRACE: I want to explain something to you. When you come
together with someone here, when you fuck, and often it
happens because you're desperate and scared half out of
your mind, you need something completely different from
your old idea of romantic fantasy. It's something less in
some ways but also more, I don't know. It's a different act.
It's almost an act of survival. There isn't much time to feel
jealousy or wish you were at the beach. And I've discovered
a loneliness here that is so deep it's almost like a drug. I
don't think there's a passion in the world that can penetrate
far enough to disturb it. And yet from time to time I find
myself reaching out . . . and something very like a ghost
slips in.

FOSTER: (*Fiddles*.) Not exactly a compliment.

GRACE: I didn't mean it anatomically.

(*Enter* JENKIN.)

JENKIN: Can you please tell me why, as soon as I produce my
credentials at Hertz, every single bloody car is miraculously
on hire? I have tried three times. Or perhaps they don't
actually own any cars here? Is it perhaps a front for some
operation? Importing Gideon Bibles or fundamentalist
sermons from the Deep South? (FOSTER *laughs*.) You may
laugh, you have a car.

(*He sits down, seems suddenly quite old*.)

FOSTER: Do you think you should be doing this, Bill?

JENKIN: I'm not doing *anything* at the moment.

FOSTER: It would be a rotten place to die.

JENKIN: It's kind of you to be so concerned. I'm perfectly all right. Just a bit tired. I find cities very tiring. I'm very worried about Mary. I need to get out of town, talk to some people.

(FOSTER *looks at* JENKIN.)

FOSTER: You've got a dodgy heart, haven't you?

JENKIN: As soon as I can steal a bicycle or a bloody llama.

FOSTER: Seriously, haven't you?

JENKIN: I renewed the batteries before I came out. I never take chances. Duracell.

(FOSTER *looks at* GRACE. *She reaches out gently for his pulse.*)

GRACE: Do you mind?

(JENKIN *leans back, his eyes half closed, fingering the spider.* GRACE *is looking at her watch.*)

FOSTER: Is this woman a close friend?

JENKIN: We met thirty odd years ago. In French Equatorial Africa. I was determined to get an interview with Schweitzer, nobody had for years. I remember my first view of the bay, when I finally got to Lambarene, was . . . rows and rows of corrugated iron huts, like a mining camp. Mary Tennant was working there as an assistant, but she was very disillusioned and wanted to leave. There was this great musician . . . theologian, giving up a brilliant career at an early age and going to care for the natives; that was the legend anyway. The truth was Schweitzer was an arrogant and stubborn man, who referred to his chosen people as *indigènes* and constantly exhorted them to *travail comme un blanc!* and whose famous hospital was depressing, filthy and unmodernized.

FOSTER: So you fucked her.

(*Pause.*)

JENKIN: We were lovers, yes . . . for a short time. She was very beautiful, she was only 25. She'd already gone through two husbands by then. The first one left her a fortune, half of which I believe she gave away and the other half she had already squandered. She seemed to have a great deal of courage, and vision, and generosity and a wonderful dry sense of humour.

26

(FLEUR *comes on. Stands uncertainly for a moment.*)

GRACE: (*Letting go of his wrist*) That seems all right. I think you just need a good night's sleep.

FLEUR: Can I join you? I ordered champagne.

JENKIN: That doesn't sound like a bad idea.

GRACE: The woman I know and the woman you describe don't sound like the same person.

JENKIN: She's not an easy person. She's certainly fearless. And sometimes complete absence of fear can be very unnerving.
(*Pause. A* WAITRESS *brings champagne.*)

FLEUR: Who are you talking about?

JENKIN: A friend of mine called Mary Tennant. She works for Christian Aid here.

FOSTER: I hope you know the price of champagne here.

JENKIN: (*Sipping*) It's extremely generous of you.

FLEUR: I wish I was fearless. Fear makes you so withdrawn and neurotic. You live in a darkness all of your own, resisting any kind of relationship with anybody, building a wall around yourself, with this fear going on and on. When we're young and have all this energy, we should be free of it, shouldn't we?

GRACE: Is there something you're scared of at the moment?

FLEUR: This country has one kind of fear, doesn't it . . . the obvious kind, but you can't begin to tackle that kind of terror until you've conquered all the other fears. The ones that stop you giving yourself to life. Does anybody understand a word I'm saying?
(*A pause.*)

JENKIN: Yes, I do. I understand you perfectly.
(FLEUR *gets up suddenly.*)

FLEUR: Excuse me . . .
(FLEUR *goes.* GRACE *puts a finger to her nose.* FOSTER *nods.* RUIZ *comes on from a different direction.*)

RUIZ: Good evening. Mr Foster, Mrs Suarez. I'm glad to find you. I have to apologize for the other night. It was bad taste joke. Forgive, eh?

FOSTER: (*Tense*) Come and join us.
(RUIZ *thinks for a second, then sits.*)

27

RUIZ: (*To* JENKIN) We have not been properly introduced, Mr Jenkin. But I know about you.

(JENKIN *mumbles a greeting, leans across the table, shakes hands.*)

Did I see Fleur? Was that Fleur sitting here? (*Slight pause.*) Yes . . . you have travelled widely. You were brave in the war. You go to Korea and even . . . North Vietnam, I believe.

JENKIN: That's true. Would you like a glass of champagne?

RUIZ: I would like to tell you about this country. People are here for such a short time and learn little about us. They have impression. Useless.

JENKIN: I agree. I'm not here to write anything. I'm here to see a friend.

RUIZ: (*To* FOSTER) You are interested in us now. Because suddenly Central America is in the news. Because suddenly there is war and threats of war and because everything United States does concerns the British, yes?

(JENKIN *gestures, a kind of agreement.*)

And suddenly there are no more jokes about banana republics.

(GRACE *gets up.*)

GRACE: Excuse me. I have to go to the bathroom.

(*She goes.*)

RUIZ: I was thinking how long she would stay at same table.

FOSTER: Neither Bill nor I are likely to make jokes about banana republics.

RUIZ: (*To* JENKIN) I'm sure you write eloquently, *estimado señor*. But from certain point of view. A man who has observe many bad things but who has always believe his way of life would survive. Am I right, señor?

JENKIN: I'm not sure I'm as optimistic as you think.

RUIZ: You are European.

JENKIN: Whatever that is, yes.

RUIZ: I am European too. My family has been here for four hundred years, no one can say they don't have any Indian blood but I tell you my friend I am ten times more Spanish than my Castilian brothers, because Spain was only country who did not expel the Jews and the Arabs. That's why they have that weakness in their blood. I have the strength of Cortés.

FOSTER: Sure. And we're Viking, Saxon, Pict, Celt, Norman, African, Jew, Asian . . .

RUIZ: (*Quietly*) That is *your* problem. You tell me what you think of my country.

(*He turns to* JENKIN.)

JENKIN: I really can't do that. I've only been here two days.

RUIZ: Then we will have . . . *impression*. (*Pause*.) Go on. Be honest.

JENKIN: I don't honestly know whether you are successful or you aren't, Señor Ruiz. Or by what criteria you want me to judge. Per capita income. The vividness of the culture. The general stock of personal happiness. The incidence of rabies.

RUIZ: I will tell you why we are not a success. Because we are not clear what we want. I am a fascist. When my ancestors conquer this new world they found something sick and dying which we should have put to sleep like an old dog. This people of human sacrifice should have been got rid of but we let them hang around our necks for these centuries like a dead, heavy thing. They would not lie down and die because they are kept alive by the memory of this old dead culture which you all find so charming.

JENKIN: And which the Ministry seems to promote with enormous relish.

RUIZ: The joke is on you. All these people are worth is covers for your beds and little stone gods to put on your bookshelves.

JENKIN: I have an aversion to little stone gods. But you're right.

RUIZ: We were girls, we put up no resistance when the Norte Americanos bought up all our land. And the same thing is happening to you. We are all little colonies.

JENKIN: But on the whole we accept it. They're our brothers. They saved us twice this century.

RUIZ: That is sentimental. The valley that runs from here for a hundred miles is so rich it could feed the whole of Central

America. You know what it is doing? Producing vegetable oil for Cassell and Cook company of USA. They are to blame for the communists. The communists are a symptom of what America does to us. So people can't deal with America, so we deal with the symptom. They get angry, they kill communists and people who want to give land to the peasants and the Indians who do not know first thing to do with it. They get angry, they kill, it is nothing personal. The Americans don't mind communists being killed. But they won't do the dirty work themselves any more. Here, or in Nicaragua. They are hypocrites! But you won't write this because it is not a nice person saying it.

JENKIN: I'm not here to write anything. I've been churning it out since 1944 and I have nothing more to say about the world except . . . (*raises his arms a little*) . . . madness!
(FOSTER *looks at* JENKIN.)

RUIZ: You reported war against Germany?

JENKIN: At the end. I was very young.

RUIZ: You feel pride? You rejoice.

JENKIN: No. Relief . . . relief, everybody did. I saw the mess we made of Berlin though. It was horrible. There was hardly a building standing. Nothing we saw at home could have prepared us for it. It was very difficult to rejoice.

RUIZ: I don't believe you. You're lying. You won. You rejoice.

JENKIN: There was no point. It was all over. The only things that were at all memorable were too bizarre to be of much interest to anybody at the time. (*A pause.*) I remember all the Allied reporters were billeted in the Am Zoo hotel. It was the only one left standing. Most of us went to official briefings by day and sat all evening in the terrible restaurant getting drunk on American beer. A few idiots were still chasing 'Hitler is Alive' stories, but they were a minority. Berlin seemed to be inhabited exclusively by starving prostitutes. There was one particularly sad and unattractive woman who used to walk up and down outside the window. She must have been at least 50 and we all agreed she was possibly the ugliest woman we had ever seen, I think she even had a glass eye. Anyway one night after a lot of beer and in a spirit of reconciliation four of us, including the austere Johnston Hope of the *Telegraph*, a man of unimpeachable rectitude, decided to ask her in to dine with us. She accepted the invitation with astonishing grace. She talked animatedly throughout the meal, told us amusing stories about the old low life of the city, flirted outrageously with all of us, greeted the terrible ersatz coffee as if it was the finest Austrian blend. It was the most courageous performance I've ever seen. But gradually I'm afraid the truth slowly dawned on us, one by one . . . that if we were not going to finally humiliate the woman . . . one of us was going to have to go to bed with her. So the meal dragged on for ever, it was excruciating. None of us could bring ourselves to say the fatal words. Then the most extraordinary thing happened. Johnston Hope. Of the *Daily Telegraph*. Stood up. And with incredible dignity, he was very tall and had a silver moustache and always carried a shooting stick, and bowed . . . courteously and said . . . 'Fraulein. It has been a delightful evening. May I have the pleasure?' And they walked through the restaurant together, as all the massed ranks of the Allied press finished their bourbon, and as they reached the door she turned and shouted, 'I chose Johnston Hope!'

(FOSTER *laughs silently. A pause.*)

RUIZ: I don't know why you tell that. It means nothing.

JENKIN: Oh, absolutely right, it's a very silly story. I suppose there's some irony there somewhere.

RUIZ: So why do you come here? Not to tell silly stories and talk to people you despise.

JENKIN: I came to see an old friend. Someone I used to admire. Unfortunately I can't trace her at the moment. She works for Christian Aid. Mary Tennant?

(GRACE *comes on,* FLEUR *behind.*)

RUIZ: These people come and go all the time. We don't need them. They come to make propaganda about infant mortality and they go home changing nothing. Our health service is improving all the time.

FLEUR: How do you improve something that doesn't exist?

RUIZ: You are making this propaganda because you think these *periodistas* will listen to you.

FLEUR: (*To* JENKIN) There's an epidemic of measles. The government radio station is broadcasting to the Indians that the vaccine we're giving them is impregnated with Fidel Castro's urine. And if they let us inject them with it their babies will grow up to be communists. (*She is looking at* GRACE *who is trying to distance herself.*)

(RUIZ *smiles, stands up, shakes his head.*)

RUIZ: (*Calm*) That was just a . . . what do you say. A fairy story. A joke. The Indians know what we mean. They don't like communists. That's why all the ones in Nicaragua come here, because the communists tell them what to do and they like to be left alone. Look, Mrs Suarez does not complain. (*To* JENKIN) Perhaps you don't understand why I care more about values of Europe than you. Maybe you should write how your Ambassador's daughter is addicted to drugs. Your readers will like. Excuse me.

(*He goes off.*)

FLEUR: (*To* JENKIN) Can we meet, tomorrow? At your hotel?

JENKIN: Of course.

GRACE: (*To* FLEUR) Let's get a cab.

FOSTER: Where are you going?

GRACE: I'll call you later. (*Protectively*) Come on.

(*They go.*)

FOSTER: I find it extremely hard to believe that you've come out here on a casual visit to look up some old boiler you screwed in Swaziland in 1950.

JENKIN: 1955.

FOSTER: I think I've told you far too much already. What are you up to, you canny old bugger?

JENKIN: I'm really not up to anything.

FOSTER: I don't believe you. Do you know what's happening here?

JENKIN: Totally lost.

FOSTER: The Americans are covering up for Ruiz. This man is a Nazi and he's swanning around at parties in the British Embassy and you know we don't put a tiny toe out of line here without American approval. Here there is an absolute crack down on any information about disappearances. And publicly a lot of media hype about this nice new democracy they've got. And the small and extremely nasty right-wing party that Ruiz leads has a handful of seats and is holding the balance of power. If he decides to pull out of a coalition it is very likely that the country would be ungovernable and the army would step in. Right? Now it's increasingly obvious that Ruiz is bad news and the Americans are both trying to distance themselves from him and keep him sweet at the same time. Do you follow me?

JENKIN: Up to a point . . .

FOSTER: The Yanks can't invade Nicaragua with a clear conscience if democracy collapses here. Their increasingly wild negotiation with people they are embarrased by, like Ruiz . . . what does it suggest to you?

JENKIN: Military intervention in Nicaragua?

FOSTER: Yes. Imminent.

FOSTER: Who the hell is this?

(*Enter* KATE ZWIMMER. *A dazzling elegant American woman who does not quite look her age.*)

JENKIN: (*Rising diffidently*) Kate . . .

ZWIMMER: What are you doing here?

JENKIN: I'm just having a bite to eat.

ZWIMMER: I can see that. I mean *here*.

JENKIN: Let me introduce . . .

ZWIMMER: I know who he is. You can't flush a toilet in this country without me knowing about it.

JENKIN: Kate. Zwimmer. (*Quiet, offhand*) The American Ambassador here.

ZWIMMER: Katherine, not Kate. I'm not a musical.

(*To* JENKIN) I've been ringing your hotel.

JENKIN: Are you alone?

ZWIMMER: That's an unusually ill-informed remark, Bill.

(JENKIN *glances round.*)

This is not a country to stroll around in. Clyde is by the door and Paul has just moved opposite us. So keep your hands on the table. (*To* FOSTER) Joke.

33

JENKIN: Mrs Zwimmer and I are old friends. Or old enemies, I'm never sure which.

ZWIMMER: Oh, now darling . . .

JENKIN: Her political career has blossomed in the last few years. Of course, it had nothing at all to do with you being in movies . . .

ZWIMMER: (*Laughs.*) You rat! (*Winks at* FOSTER.) I must have a drink or I'll die.

JENKIN: What *were* your screen credits, I'm sorry. I always forget them.

ZWIMMER: (*Genially*) You rat. You always were such a rat. Excuse me.

(*She waves offstage.* FOSTER *looks at* JENKIN *who gives the faintest flicker of a smile.* RUIZ *bounds on, enthusiastically.*)

RUIZ: Mrs Zwimmer! How lovely to see you.

ZWIMMER: I'll have a large bourbon. And what do you guys want?

(RUIZ *stops as if winded. There is a dreadful pause.*)

JENKIN: (*With instinctive tact*) Señor Ruiz has been telling us all about the situation here.

(ZWIMMER *takes in the situation with the tiniest movement of the head.*)

ZWIMMER: Find me a waiter, Raul, there's a doll. You're looking very handsome today.

RUIZ: (*Tightly*) Of course.

(RUIZ *exits without a flicker.* JENKIN *is enjoying himself,* FOSTER *doesn't appear to quite believe what he's seeing.*)

ZWIMMER: He *was* a waiter too. He should have stayed one. They don't as a rule make good politicians. Look at Ho Chi Minh.

JENKIN: I don't know, I thought Ho made quite a good fist of it.

ZWIMMER: Waiters know too much. They are in the restaurant *and* in the kitchen. It's not healthy.

JENKIN: All I can say is he was very good company.

ZWIMMER: When Bill became bored with writing doom-laded reports about the carnage of war, he took to cultivating heads of state, usually disreputable and on the Left . . . like a sort of International Court Jester, aren't you, dear?

34

JENKIN: You, of course, only mix with men of honesty and rectitude. I imagine that's why you came here.

ZWIMMER: I didn't come here, dear, I was sent.

(JENKIN *impassive*.)

(*To* FOSTER) I suppose you're too young to have seen any of my films.

FOSTER: No . . . I've seen at least two . . . no, three. Er . . . *Heaven Sent*, *The Pharoahs* and . . .

ZWIMMER: *The End of Town?*

JENKIN: (*To* FOSTER, *quickly*) That's it. You've got them all.

FOSTER: No, that wasn't the one . . .

JENKIN: I was always a bit hazy about the details. I remember a bath in asses' milk, and a rather suggestive swim across the swollen Missouri in a wet shirt.

ZWIMMER: I was not a starlet, Bill.

JENKIN: You were not a star.

ZWIMMER: I've never claimed to be as big as Day or Heyworth.

JENKIN: You *fucked* a lot of stars.

ZWIMMER: (*Laughs*.) I gave all that up a long time ago. I don't know what Kissinger meant when he said power is the greatest aphrodisiac. Frankly I prefer power straight, without the trimmings. Where's that waiter? (*Waves impatiently*.) Bill, I'm sorry to see you looking so frail. I'd heard you'd made a good recovery. I'm going to have you round to tea and we can talk about old times. (*Looks off*.) There's a waiter waving. (*To* JENKIN) You have a phone call, I think.

JENKIN: (*Scrambling up*) Excuse me.

(*He goes off*. FOSTER *tries to see what he's doing*.)

ZWIMMER: I can see you're very competitive, Mr Foster. Perhaps we always are, with our mentors.

FOSTER: I'm here to write a book. Bill's on holiday.

ZWIMMER: (*Shakes her head disbelievingly*.) You needn't worry, he isn't speeding off to follow a *new lead*. I fixed up the phone call so we could be alone together. I believe you've been carrying out your own little investigation about this woman.

FOSTER: Some bloodstained clothing was found near where she disappeared.

ZWIMMER: A shoe, You found it. Clever boy. Why didn't you hand it over to the police?

FOSTER: I did.

ZWIMMER: You should have done it straight away.

FOSTER: I wanted to get it identified by her colleagues.

ZWIMMER: What you did could make you an accessory here.

FOSTER: It looks fairly obvious that she's been murdered.

ZWIMMER: There's no body. There's usually a body here. *Pour encourager les autres*. We know certain facts about Mrs T. She may have left the country in a hurry.

FOSTER: Gone to Nicaragua. As they say.

ZWIMMER: You're a bright boy. I can see.

FOSTER: You'll have to release the facts eventually.

ZWIMMER: We may decide not to release them. For reasons of security. You think you can make a good story if you can dig up some political scandal over her death, if she's dead. Am I right?

FOSTER: I think perhaps you've got my politics confused.

ZWIMMER: No. I think I read you right. If you give us time to do everything we have to do. Three days, maybe. Then I'll brief you fully on all the facts. And give you clearance.

FOSTER: With respect. No journalist could possibly accept those terms. Jenkin hasn't accepted the conditions. He says he has a personal connection with this woman.

ZWIMMER: Does he? He probably owes her money.

FOSTER: I'm sorry . . . He's not going to stop asking questions whether there's a body or not.

ZWIMMER: Bill Jenkin is not known for his objectivity. He is an anti-American. (*Pause.*) I give you my solemn promise that I will tell you everything we find out. Our intelligence gathering is very sophisticated here.

FOSTER: I'll have to think about it.

ZWIMMER: I spoke to your proprietor yesterday. He was full of praise for your reporting. You know that he isn't very trusting of foreign correspondents.

(FOSTER *picks up the threat.* RUIZ *enters with a double bourbon on a tray.*)

(*Seeing* RUIZ) Raul. Now the joke's on me. You're very kind.

36

(RUIZ *makes to put the drink down, but instead throws it in* ZWIMMER's *face. He turns on his heel and walks out. The band stops playing.*)
(*With unearthly composure*) And now it looks as if the bourbon's on me.
(*The band begins again.*)
(*Smiles off.*) He was probably a fifth of a second from getting a bullet in the back. What a tribute to discipline and training. You really would have had something to write about. (*Gets up, flicking a few droplets from a sleeve.*) *Hasta luego*, Sebastian. We'll keep in touch.
(*She goes. Music up as light fades on* FOSTER.)

Night sounds. Blue tropical night.
GRACE: (*Off*) Watch the edge!
FLEUR: (*Off*) I can't see anything!
(GRACE *comes on.*)
GRACE: It's easy if you watch the line of trees!
(FLEUR *comes on.*)
(*Smiling*) You're quite fit for a junkie.
(FLEUR *sits down*, GRACE *joins her.*)
FLEUR: I just want to make it clear to you that I don't give a damn about revolutions and I'm not particularly fond of Nicaragua. I found it boring. Like an enormous primary school and all the teachers really *positive*. Not to mention the endless foreign delegations. So if that's a requirement of your friendship I'm warning you in advance.
GRACE: What makes you think I'm on their side? Though I have to say after five years here that all the things you describe sound like heaven to me.
FLEUR: Why are you being so friendly? What do you want?
GRACE: How did you get hooked on smack?
FLEUR: My father was British Consul in Marseilles when I was 15. I got in with some people there. When my parents found out they sent me off to finishing school but I kept running away. When they came out here I stayed in London or LA, did a bit of modelling. That got harder. After a time it gets more and more difficult to hide the

37

spots. Then I did odd jobs for film companies, lost them all. Then clinics. In and out of clinics . . . endless therapy. It's all sort of worked really. Apparently there's this day when you suddenly wake up and know you're back in the world again. It hasn't happened yet.

GRACE: It looks to me as if you're slipping back very fast.

FLEUR: She's dead.

GRACE: Who is?

FLEUR: That woman.

GRACE: How do you know?

FLEUR: I know. Instinct.

(*Pause*.)

GRACE: Can I help you? I mean is there something. . . ?

FLEUR: Do you know about the philosophy of Eternal Return? If we die and we disappear for ever and never return, we have no substance at all, we're just ghosts. And everything we did however terrible or glorious or foolish means absolutely nothing. It hasn't any weight. It means that because things fade away they are always eternally forgiven. Forgiven first and then forgotten. Like two people five hundred years ago who considered themselves more in love than any two people had ever been and one betrayed the other or a useless battle in Mesopotamia that never changed anything.

GRACE: That's incredibly bleak.

FLEUR: But if everything we do recurs an infinite number of times, every action we take has a massive weight and responsibility. It is always there like a cliff in front of us. We have to keep repeating and repeating it. No escape. No excuses. No nostalgia.

GRACE: Isn't that just a cute way of saying we must take responsibility for everything we do?

FLEUR: Oh, maybe.

GRACE: When you've been here for a while you have responsibilities. And loyalties. And what is true today isn't true tomorrow. It's sad to say it, but the truth doesn't belong to everyone by right. Christmas cracker motto. Everything you learn, you gotta earn.

38

FLEUR: The moon is made of Gorgonzola, the rivers run
backwards and the volcanoes were borrowed from
Disneyland. It's cold up here. Shall we go?

GRACE: (*Getting up*) Sure. Do you want to sleep on the couch?
It'll save you a journey.

FLEUR: (*Standing*) Thank you. (*Looks out. Shakes her head
slowly.*) It happened down there. In Felicidad.

GRACE: What makes you think that?

FLEUR: I know. Do you? You do. You know everything.
(GRACE *starts to move.*)

GRACE: Let's go. I'm getting cold too.
(*They go as the lights fade.*)

Before FLEUR *and* GRACE *have left the stage, sunlight once again
streams through the church door and* JENKIN *comes on, half running,
half staggering, his shirt covered in blood and a bloody cloth
wrapped around the side of his head.*

JENKIN: I'm bleeding to death!

RIGOBERTO: (*Off*) No cause for panic.
(*The light from the door gradually narrows, leaving just
dappled light. The door bangs shut.*)

JENKIN: I'm bleeding to death!
(*A bolt draws shut.*)

RIGOBERTO: (*On*) I think in the circumstances we'll keep the
door bolted.

JENKIN: Yes, for heaven's sake, yes.

RIGOBERTO: I keep a first aid supply in the . . . (*searches for the
word*) . . . vestry.

JENKIN: I'll come with you.

RIGOBERTO: (*Sharply*) No . . . I won't be a minute.
(RIGOBERTO *goes off quickly.* JENKIN *takes a small bottle of
clear spirit from his jacket pocket and takes a long gulp.*)

JENKIN: (*Crossing himself*) In nomine patris et filii et spiritus
sancti.
(*He slips the bottle back.* RIGOBERTO *emerges with a first aid
box.*)

RIGOBERTO: You really ought to go to the hospital. But I think
it would be safer to stay here for a while. (*Unwrapping the*

39

cloth) You have not lost the whole ear. It's a clean cut.

JENKIN: That's very reassuring.

RIGOBERTO: I should never have left you alone. (*Methodically unpacks the things from the first aid box.*) Now tell me real what happen.

JENKIN: I went to get a drink from the bar, very English habit. There was a man by the bar who'd been staring at us all the time, you couldn't see him because you had your back to him. He was tubby, with a green T-shirt, with the name of a baseball team on it. He put his hand rather heavily on my shoulder and said something like, well I think he meant are you a friend of the priest. I heard the words *padre* and *amigo*. I said, 'Yes, I was a very good friend of yours.' His response was to produce what looked like a miniature butcher's cleaver and chop my bloody ear off.

RIGOBERTO: (*Opening a bottle of iodine*) This is going to hurt.

JENKIN: Then he followed it up with a lot of silkily delivered abuse in which the word *Marxeest* figured prominently, as well as sundry invitations to go home. I told him I was not a Marxist.

RIGOBERTO: It fell on deaf . . . I'm sorry. Well they are obviously not ready to kill us yet. So we can be thankful. Are you ready? (*Holds up the iodine-soaked lint.*) I will tell you a joke. From a Polish priest I met in America. There are two dogs. One Czech one Pole. They meet at Polish–Czech border. They are crossing into each other's country. Czech dog cannot believe this of the Polish dog. Why you want to come to my country? Because I want to eat, say the Polish dog. Why you want to come to my country? Because I want to bark, say the Czech dog. (*He slams the iodine-soaked dressing round* JENKIN'*s ear and begins to bandage his head.*)

JENKIN: Jesus Christ! Sorry.

RIGOBERTO: I thought it was a good joke. Do you want another? I only know Polish jokes. After killing of Popiełuszko, local priest in small Polish village is hitch-hiking on road. His friend local policeman comes up on motor bike. 'Do you want a lift, father?' 'No, thank you,' says priest, 'I can't swim.'

(JENKIN *winces again*.)

That will keep the gangrene out for a few hours.

(*He finishes tying the bandage*.)

JENKIN: I believe everything you've told me about this place.

RIGOBERTO: I'm very sorry you are involved. But perhaps it is good for you. Perhaps you don't mind.

(JENKIN *looks suddenly tired and leans back against the bench*.)

JENKIN: What did you tell Foster when you saw him?

RIGOBERTO: Nothing. I read him some poetry. I am a poet too. Would you like to hear?

JENKIN: I don't want to listen to bloody poetry! I need some information from you.

RIGOBERTO: (*A smile*.) I'm sorry I didn't take your questions seriously. We were drinking. Which is a serious business as I know you think too. I don't normally get such a good chance to enjoy myself with someone who knows the world and has so many good stories to tell. So you have to forgive me. I left you alone not knowing you were in any danger. But to laugh is the best thing in the world, isn't it? Laughter is a divine gift. Some of my brothers in the church don't like it too much. Maybe all our problems in Latin America are connected with this. I will maybe explore this sometime.

JENKIN: I have not come here to coldly investigate a missing person and write a story. I have no *career ambitions* left. It's personal, do you understand? Private.

(JENKIN *is holding the brass tarantula*.)

RIGOBERTO: May I see?

(*He examines it carefully*. JENKIN *watches him*.)

JENKIN: (*Takes out a small folder of Polaroid snaps*.) I was given these snaps of an Amnesty International benefit in Belize. That's Mary Tennant. And that's you there, isn't it? And there? *Comprensivo*. The two of you. I would say.

RIGOBERTO: You want to find this rabid parrot called truth or something, yes? There is no such thing here. Everything is touched by mystery. It only deepens the urgency of our work.

41

JENKIN: With great respect. (*Vehemently*) Bullshit. Unfortunately for you I wasn't born yesterday.

RIGOBERTO: (*Explosively*) Why do you meddle, you stupid old man? For four centuries we ask same question. Why don't you leave us *alone*?

(*There is a loud knocking on the door.*)

I think they're probably ready to kill us now. Don't worry. They can't get in. And they don't know for certain we're here.

(*The knocking continues, with a strange rhythm this time. Not so loud.*)

Oh, I am mad. What is today? The nineteenth?

(*He starts to go to the door.*)

JENKIN: I really am a complete coward. I'm not at all ready to be shot to pieces. For God's sake don't let anybody in.

RIGOBERTO: I must. It is St Sebastian.

(JENKIN *sits, with a small helpless gesture.* RIGOBERTO *is transfigured by excitement.*)

Whatever you do, don't interfere. Watch and do nothing.

(*The door opens again. Chanting and music from outside, celebratory.*)

Bienvenido, ninos!

(*Lights fade.*)

ACT TWO

JENKIN *moves into a spot.*

JENKIN: It happened in Felicidad. It was unremarkable. The woman looked *tranquilo*. The men had clean white shirts. Nobody noticed anything unusual. Just one mad old woman who sits in the shade every morning in front of her house. She told me that when the men approached the Englishwoman, the children ran away.

The church, dappled light. Lights grow around JENKIN.

RIGOBERTO *is at the door.*

RIGOBERTO: Bienvenido! Bienvenido! Bienvenido!
(NORA *and* RONOS, *another Indian, come quietly into the church. They are barefoot and are wearing clay masks. They ignore* JENKIN *and* RIGOBERTO *and move downstage. They stand in front of the statue of the Virgin Mary.*)

NORA: (*Conversationally*) Confesakuspaqa curamansi juchanchistaqa saquenpunchis.

RONOS: Chay jinaqa jayk'a runaq juchan q'epiykusqacha kashan.

RIGOBERTO: (*In a whisper, to* JENKIN) She says, 'When we make our confession we get rid of all their sins to the priest.' He says, 'If that is so think how many sins he must be carrying.'
(*The two Indians have knelt in front of the Virgin, and are unwrapping a cloth. They bundle the statue up in the cloth and carry her off.*)

JENKIN: They're stealing her.

RIGOBERTO: (*With a smile*) Yes, they're stealing her.

NORA: (*Off*) Juchanchista q'eperanpusunchis!
(*Offstage the music stops. The crowd repeats the shout. Then the music begins again. The crowd is moving off.*)

JENKIN: What did she say?

RIGOBERTO: Let us give up our sins.

JENKIN: Are they going to bring her back?

43

RIGOBERTO: We will follow them for a bit. I am not really
    allowed to watch, but if we keep out of sight it's all right.
    It's quite safe.
JENKIN: Oh, yes, yes. I'm sure. Let's go then.
    (*They go off together,* JENKIN *reluctantly. The lights dim.*)

*The sound of parakeets. And wind. Lights come up again. The
Christ in the distance.* FOSTER *is lying on his back near the seat.*
GRACE *comes on.*
FOSTER: Any sign?
GRACE: No. She might be coming up another path.
FOSTER: Nobody is ever on time here.
GRACE: Remember she's risking her life talking to you.
FOSTER: I'm probably risking my life talking to her.
    (*They embrace.* NORA *enters. She waits patiently. They break
    apart, calm.* FOSTER *stands.*)
    Buenas días.
NORA: (*A nod.*) Buenas días. We met before.
GRACE: Nora. Buenas días. (*In Spanish*) Señor Foster has come
    to talk to you. He is a good man. He knows about the
    relatives of the Disappeared. He will publicize the cases. So
    tell him what happened to your family.
    (NORA *starts speaking in Spanish.*)
    (*Translating*) My first boy, Miguel, was kidnapped by six
    men in hoods. That was on April thirteenth this year . . .
    (NORA *continues in Spanish,* GRACE *translates it into English
    for* FOSTER *every three or four sentences.*)
    They had very sophisticated weapons. The kind only the
    military have. At dawn, the house was surrounded . . .
    There were helicopters going over the roof. Some of the
    cars outside didn't have licence plates. Only the military
    are allowed to do that. This is the third time they've taken
    him. The last time, they just beat him up . . . They left
    him for dead by the road . . . I'm sure he is dead like Noel
    and Tomas. With Tomas they killed him openly and gave
    me his head as a final warning . . . but the other two had
    never been politically active.
FOSTER: Does she think the same people killed Mrs Tennant?

(NORA *has begun again.*)

GRACE: (*Holds up a hand to* FOSTER.) My friend Juana
    Mercado's daughter was detained only because she had
    travelled through Nicaragua from Costa Rica. She has
    exhausted all legal means of trying to find out where she is.

FOSTER: Well, perhaps I ought to speak to Juana herself.
    (NORA *continues.*)

GRACE: Listen to what she has to say.

FOSTER: Ask her if she knew Mary Tennant.

GRACE: (*Translating*) . . . her name was not on the detainee
    list . . .

FOSTER: You know, Mrs Tennant?

NORA: Que?

GRACE: (*In Spanish*) He's asking you if you know an
    Englishwoman. (*To* FOSTER) This woman has come to talk
    about her sons. She doesn't have a lot of time.

NORA: Que?

FOSTER: Mary Tennant. Inglés?

NORA: Sí.

FOSTER: She knows her. (*To* GRACE) Ask her if she knows who
    killed her.

GRACE: She's here to talk about people who have disappeared.
    (NORA *watches patiently.*)

FOSTER: I know, I'll do my best to publicize that, but ask . . .
    her if she knows anything at all about Mary Tennant. Any
    little detail.

GRACE: (*In Spanish*) Sorry. It's rude to interrupt you. He wants to
    know if you know anything at all about what happened to her.
    (GRACE *looks bleakly at* FOSTER *as* NORA *talks in Spanish
    again.*)

NORA: (*Finishing*) . . . una amigo de Padre Bravo. Una buena
    mujer. Ella gustaria pelear.

GRACE: (*Translating*) I know her. I know she was around about
    two weeks ago because she brought presents for the
    children outside the church. That was the last time I saw
    her. She is a friend of . . . (*Stops translating.*)

FOSTER: Why did you stop? She said something about being a
    friend of Father Bravo. A fighter. . . ?

45

GRACE: You misheard her. Do you want me to carry on or not?
(*A pause.* NORA *looks at* GRACE.)
(*In Spanish*) You must tell us more about the disappeared.
(NORA *begins again.*)
FOSTER: That's what she said. Why didn't you translate that?
GRACE: (*Translating*) As far as my sons go, I have presented six
Habeas Corpus writs and spent months in legal proceedings
. . . All this has made me ill. I have been very depressed.
FOSTER: Tell her I'll do everything I can to publicize their case.
Perhaps she would give me the names of people who are
missing?
GRACE: (*In Spanish*) The names. Of the Disappeared.
(NORA *produces a piece of paper and hands it over to* FOSTER.
FOSTER *immediately puts it in his pocket.*)
FOSTER: Thank you. Before she goes. Would you ask her if she
knows anybody else who might have seen Mrs Tennant that
day.
GRACE: Before she *goes*.
FOSTER: It must be pretty risky to hang about with us.
GRACE: She's only just begun.
FOSTER: Listen, I don't have a lot of space. This will give me
enough for the moment. Ask her if she knows anyone.
GRACE: (*Furiously*) No. (*Pause.*) You ask her.
(NORA *waits.* FOSTER *looks pleadingly then throws himself into
the task.*)
FOSTER: (*In bad Spanish*) You know . . . person who knows
person . . . seeing well Mrs Tennant . . . on that day.
Important for information . . . political badness. Find
contact who is seeing.
(NORA *looks at* GRACE, *not understanding what is going on, or
being said.* GRACE *is impenetrable.*)
You know. You know . . .
(NORA *shrugs. Looks at* GRACE. GRACE *shakes her head
sadly.*)
(*To* GRACE) Please.
GRACE: No.
NORA: (*Standing*) Muchas gracias, señor. (*To* GRACE) Muchas
gracias.

(FOSTER *turns his back and flings his arms up in a gesture of frustration.*)

Buenas días.

(NORA *goes.*)

FOSTER: (*Studying*) Shall we go?

GRACE: I'll make my own way back. My car's in the village.

FOSTER: I'll give you a lift there.

GRACE: Those people were human beings. You can write things that can't be said in the papers here. It has an effect.

FOSTER: Most people don't give a damn. I wish they did. But they don't. They're interested in weightier things.

GRACE: Weighty? (*Stares at him.*) You people fuck so lightly. (*She goes. A pause.* FOSTER *picks up some binoculars. Focuses. The lights change.*)

The church. Evening. JENKIN *and* RIGOBERTO.

RIGOBERTO: (*Lighting a candle*) That was an education, yes?

JENKIN: (*Fiddling with his bandage*) What on earth do they do with the Virgin?

RIGOBERTO: Leave the bandage alone. You will get an infection if you don't take care. Who knows what they do with her? Maybe they fuck in the fields at the full moon and she watches them. This has been going on for a hundred years. They always bring her back.

JENKIN: (*Producing a folded newspaper from his jacket*) One of your newspapers has published an article about you. It's by Bishop Castillo.

RIGOBERTO: (*Going to look briefly over* JENKIN's *shoulder*) El Nuevo Tiempo, they love me. Ayayay! Look how they've touched the picture up to make it look like I'm growing a beard like Fidel Castro.

JENKIN: You seem to be in a bit of trouble with the Vatican?

RIGOBERTO: There are thousands of priests in Latin America in trouble with the Vatican. We are on the side of the poor.

JENKIN: Class struggle, in other words.

RIGOBERTO: My friend, I don't get too many landowners coming here. They don't come to confession and tell me that they've just thrown some *campesino* out of his house

47

and beaten up his son. My congregation lives below subsistence level. This is the poorest country in Latin America. But believe me if the others came to me I would help them. Willingly. But we give preference to the poor because they are preferred by God. This is a requirement of charity which is part of the Christian teaching.

JENKIN: It says in the article you have attacked the authority of the Pope and the recent edicts of the Vatican.

RIGOBERTO: (*Quietly, emphatically*) They are liars. I would never attack him. Never. I love John Paul. But he has very bad influences in Rome. I want him to have greater freedom in his mission. He's a prisoner in the Vatican. They think it is all right for the Church to be against the State in Poland but here, or in Guatemala where there are Indians being massacred by the army, it is not so good to take sides. I disagree with the hierarchy of the Church.

JENKIN: On matters of faith?

RIGOBERTO: I will not discuss matters of faith with you! Why are you too so keen to prove I am a revolutionary? What are you, señor?

JENKIN: I'm probably a figure of fun these days: a socialist, a democrat, a humanist, a pacifist. Rather quaint, something quite peripheral and outdated.

RIGOBERTO: These are all fine things to be. Why do you say them as if they're a disease you have? I don't understand you people. We look to you people for a lead. Why don't you shout about it. Humanist! Pacifist! Socialist! Democrat! (RIGOBERTO *is angry, turns his back.*)

JENKIN: It's not altogether my style to shout. But if you read . . .

RIGOBERTO: (*Turning*) I'm sorry that I cannot help you about Mrs Tennant. I think she was probably robbed and murdered and they got rid of the body.

JENKIN: And left the bloodstained shoe to draw attention to it.

RIGOBERTO: On the other hand I do not think the government here would be so silly as to kill an Englishwoman. (*Slight pause.*) They have their hands full killing their own people.

48

JENKIN: There's a very old woman in the *barrio* who saw her
walking with two men. And she said minutes before you
and Mrs Tennant were talking together in the street. Then
some children came up. She said there were two shots. She
said she saw you running. Rosario . . .

RIGOBERTO: She's a mad old woman. Did you give her money?
(*Throwing up his arms*) You don't understand these people.
(JENKIN *for the first time looks defeated. He takes out a
handkerchief and mops his brow, fiddles with his bandage.*)

JENKIN: I'm a little tired. (*Fiddles again.*)

RIGOBERTO: (*Sharply*) Don't do that. You'll get an infection.
You must go to hospital tomorrow.

JENKIN: I must go. If I can.

RIGOBERTO: I will not let you move until you have rested.
(*Banging on the door.*)
I have to go, I'm sorry. I'm expecting friends. I would like
you to hide. Go under the altar.
(JENKIN *dumbfounded.*)
Quick.
(*He goes to the door.* JENKIN *off. Lights down.*)

*The American flag is flown in. Appropriate music as it is lowered to
half-mast.* JENKIN, FLEUR *and* ZWIMMER. JENKIN *without
bandage.*

ZWIMMER: I'm sorry to have kept you waiting so long. (*Sitting,
gesturing the others to sit*) I thought our meeting was going to
be *à deux*. (*To* FLEUR) I'd rather hoped to talk to Mr
Jenkin in private. Mr Jenkin and I are old friends. We first
met at a party in Washington to celebrate President
Kennedy's victory. He was quite barbarically drunk.

JENKIN: So were you. As I remember.

ZWIMMER: I'm sorry this is very rude of us.
(FLEUR *turns to* JENKIN *for direction.*)

JENKIN: (*To* ZWIMMER) I'm sure she'll find it fascinating.

ZWIMMER: I don't have to prolong this meeting, you know.

JENKIN: We have waited four hours. There are, as I think you
know, communication possibilities with regard to factual
updating which may be mutually edifying. We have enough

evidence to initiate a proper inquiry. To the effect that Mrs Tennant was murdered by two men, off-duty soldiers, and that the killing was ordered directly by the Ministry of the Interior. Raul Ruiz, in fact.

ZWIMMER: Bill, this is rather an insensitive time to be flying a kite. There is no body.

JENKIN: I've brought Miss Buchanan here because she has told me certain facts. I can't prove that what she says is the truth. But at the moment I find her story convincing. Enough to mount a proper investigation.

ZWIMMER: That's up to them. (*To* FLEUR) You have something to tell me?

FLEUR: Yes . . .

ZWIMMER: Before you go any further, as a British citizen is involved, I think there is someone else who ought to hear your story. (*Presses a buzzer.*) Would you ask Mr Buchanan to join us?

FLEUR: No!

ZWIMMER: I think your father should hear what you have to say. He probably knows if you're telling the truth better than any of us.

FLEUR: (*Standing*) I'm going.

JENKIN: Were you telling me the truth?

FLEUR: Yes!

(BUCHANAN *comes on*.)

But I can't. In front of him.

JENKIN: Then no one will possibly believe you.

BUCHANAN: (*To* ZWIMMER) This is an impossible situation for me, Kate.

ZWIMMER: I think we should sort this out now, Charlie. Unless you have any other ideas. Do you?

(BUCHANAN *shakes his head. Sits. A pause.*)

JENKIN: Go on. You can't back out now. You haven't done anything wrong.

(JENKIN *turns to* FLEUR.)

FLEUR: (*Head lowered*) Ruiz and I were lovers.

ZWIMMER: Really?

FLEUR: Yes, I . . .

50

(*Pause.*)

BUCHANAN: (*Gently*) Go on.

FLEUR: He took me to the Hyatt. He keeps a suite there. Where he conducts his affairs. And his business.

ZWIMMER: We know about the affairs. I'm surprised you didn't.

FLEUR: He'd been OK the night before but in the morning he was different. He started drinking as soon as he got up. I wanted to leave but he wouldn't let me. I was getting very frightened. About ten o'clock there was a knock on the door. These two quite young blokes came in. They had clean shirts on but I noticed that one of the boys had a patch of caked blood right down the sides of his trousers.

BUCHANAN: Anything else?

FLEUR: I think the other one had blood on his shoes. Raul pushed me off into the bedroom, I listened. They had a conversation in Spanish. There was a lot of laughing. They said, 'We killed the Englishwoman.' Raul said, 'Where did you find the bitch?' They said, 'In Felicidad. She went to see her friend the priest. We waited until she was on her own then we took her for a little walk. We told her we knew who had stolen her precious milk.' Raul laughed at this. I was so scared, I pretended I'd been asleep. He came in and told me to go. He asked for my telephone number but I wouldn't give it to him. About two days later he managed to track me down.

ZWIMMER: I find it hard to believe he didn't know who you were.

FLEUR: I told him I was a student.

ZWIMMER: Can you put a date on this?

FLEUR: It was thirteen days ago. The fifth of June.

ZWIMMER: Thank you.

(*She makes a note.*)

FLEUR: We met again. From then on he's been threatening me constantly. I've made a detailed statement about what I've heard and there's a copy lodged with the police and a lawyer here.

JENKIN: They seem rather reluctant to do anything about it.

BUCHANAN: Why didn't you tell me about this?

ZWIMMER: I think I'd like to talk to Mr Jenkin alone. And perhaps you'd like to talk to your daughter, Charlie?

FLEUR: I'll stay, thank you. I've said all I want to say.

BUCHANAN: (*To* FLEUR) Will you come with me for a minute. (*Pause.*) Please. I think you owe it to me.
(FLEUR *turns to* JENKIN.)

JENKIN: (*To* FLEUR) It's all right. Wait for me outside.
(FLEUR *goes.* BUCHANAN *follows.*)

ZWIMMER: Bill, believe me, it would be far less embarrassing for me if your story was true. If I could put the whole thing into reverse I would. But the thing looks open and shut to me.

JENKIN: A case of my opening and you shutting.

ZWIMMER: I don't think that's fair. This girl has been a heroin addict. Ruiz obviously jilted her and she wants to get back at him. She's just a spoilt little minx who enjoys playing dangerous games. I can't believe a reporter of your reputation could be taken in by such nonsense.
(*Pause.*)

JENKIN: Kate, you may not have ever been a junkie but you have never had a great capacity for factuality. The longer I'm confronted with official lies, the more stubborn it makes me.

ZWIMMER: You're not a well man. You have by all accounts a delightful family. You're not short of money. You have a fine reputation. You have nothing to prove.

JENKIN: Oh, absolutely.

ZWIMMER: There is no more potential in this. Give up and go home. That you should come all this way and risk your health not to mention your reputation on a wild goose chase. This place is crawling with people ready to tell tall stories to the gullible about disappearances. Anybody would think there was no murder, robbery, assault or any kind of common or garden violence that wasn't . . . political. It's the old Marxist trick.

JENKIN: Marxists! Where are the bloody Marxists? There are more Marxists in the London School of Economics than there are in the whole country.

ZWIMMER: This is a very small country and the London School of Economics is a very big college.

(*A pause.*)

You remember that party when we first met? You tried to hump me. It was rather a good party. Don't you remember?

(*Slight pause.*)

JENKIN: I remember the party.

ZWIMMER: What do you remember?

JENKIN: I remember your future husband was unconscious. We drove to Virginia Beach in a Dodge convertible and watched the dawn come up.

ZWIMMER: (*Smiling, shaking her head*) You don't remember you tried to hump me? You've forgotten that?

JENKIN: That wasn't quite how I remember it. (*Standing*) I ought to go.

ZWIMMER: (*Stays sitting.*) You've become anti-American, Bill. That puts you on the sidelines. You are no longer credible.

JENKIN: Some of my dearest friends are American, Kate. Some of the most principled reporters I've ever met. The very best people.

ZWIMMER: You're dodging what I said. Your Vietnam reports were anti-American. They were not objective.

JENKIN: I remember how tenderly and painstakingly the American army taught Vietnamese children to walk on artificial legs. It was hard sometimes to remember that it was you that blew them away in the first place.

ZWIMMER: When I saw you here I began to think history was repeating itself.

JENKIN: Is history repeating itself?

ZWIMMER: The only question for America is whether we have the determination and strength to carry through what we know to be right.

JENKIN: That's something we have in common.

ZWIMMER: (*Standing*) In fifty years' time the people of this country are going to thank us for saving them from communist tyranny.

JENKIN: Whether they like it or not.

53

(ZWIMMER *smiles, fiddles with her hair.*)

ZWIMMER: You did try to hump me.

JENKIN: That's your story.

ZWIMMER: You see. You've wiped it out. It must be the thought of once wanting a liaison with such an old Republican.

JENKIN: I wouldn't be ashamed of that. I've met some good Republicans.

ZWIMMER: You tried. You did.

JENKIN: I think it's your memory that's at fault, Kate.

ZWIMMER: You threw yourself at me. In an upstairs bedroom. You definitely tried. I don't forget these things.
(*A pause.*)

JENKIN: I've always been under the impression I succeeded. (*Slight pause.*) But then it was a long time ago. (*Another pause.*)

ZWIMMER: It can't have meant very much. I've forgotten it.

JENKIN: I'll show myself out then. But I think I should tell you before I go what my real interest in Mary Tennant is. I met Mary when I'd been married for ten years to my first wife. How can I put it . . . clumsily . . . she was the one, the most important one and though I'm getting old and I'm inordinately happily married . . . still is. I don't know whether you understand.

ZWIMMER: (*Laughing*) You stupid old man. What are you going to do now?

JENKIN: I'm going to see a priest.

ZWIMMER: Because of a friendship between us that was real enough at the time, and an affection . . . which is still real, I strongly advise you not to go any further. I'm sure you understand what I mean.

JENKIN: I never understand a word you say Kate. The *Times* crossword is easier to decipher. Goodbye.
(JENKIN *goes.* ZWIMMER *sits back in a chair.* BUCHANAN *comes on.*)

BUCHANAN: Kate, I have to say . . . that I believe my daughter's story, and I shall stand by her. For family reasons.

ZWIMMER: I understand. (*Stands.*) I've enjoyed the years we've worked together. We've worked together closely.

BUCHANAN: Yes. It was very pleasant.

ZWIMMER: I think you should think again. And think about your career.

BUCHANAN: I already have. But thank you for saying what you did.

(*The flag flies out. The lights change. The star spangled banner.*)

The church. The knocking again. RUIZ *comes on ahead of* RIGOBERTO. *He is drunk but not aggressively so. Bulge of shoulder holster visible.*

RIGOBERTO: (*In Spanish*) You haven't been to confession lately, Raul.

RUIZ: (*In Spanish*) I go to the Bishop now.

RIGOBERTO: (*In English, and thereafter*) The Bishop. Do you?

RUIZ: I am a famous person. (*Sits down.*) Minister of Interior vice. (*Giggles.*)

RIGOBERTO: I hope you tell the Bishop everything.

RUIZ: The Bishop is very worried about you, Rigoberto. He thinks if there are too many priests like you in our country, John Paul won't make him a cardinal.

RIGOBERTO: (*With a smile*) Tell him to have faith.

RUIZ: It is a bad business this Americano killing these women. They are animals. I wish they would go and kill a few Sandinistas in Nicaragua.

RIGOBERTO: You killed this woman, Raul.

RUIZ: (*With a roar of laughter*) Me!

RIGOBERTO: This was not done by any North American. Nor these disappearances.

RUIZ: How can you be so sure, father? Have you got a hot line to God, now? Eh? Why do you think you're so much cleverer than me? We go to the same school. We come from the same blood. But only one of us loves his country. Does that mean he doesn't know anything, father?

RIGOBERTO: God is all forgiving. Even for murderers.

RUIZ: Nobody kills no one for no reason. (*Pause.*) Do you want to be a martyr?

55

RIGOBERTO: That is up to God.

RUIZ: I am worried about your God, father. He worries me a great deal. I think perhaps he signed a pact with Fidel Castro. He doesn't seem to worry about people's souls any more. Unless people keep their souls in their bellies. Or their pay packets. I think your God needs to be talked to, father. I think when you get on your hot line, you should ask him what he's up to, eh? (*Pause,* RUIZ *goes and puts an arm on* RIGOBERTO'S *shoulder.*)

Don't take it to heart, father.

RIGOBERTO: I am not. You are very confused, Raul. You have a bad conscience.

RUIZ: You're a good man, father. You are a hard worker. You look after people. It's all right.

RIGOBERTO: Would you like to confess yours sins to me?

RUIZ: (*Slyly*) Not from a communist.

RIGOBERTO: I am not a communist.

RUIZ: I believe you, my friend. I hope John Paul will believe you too. (*Turns on* RIGOBERTO, *suddenly furious.*) You think entertaining foreign journalists is going to give you any protection? You haven't any protection now, have you?

RIGOBERTO: What do I need protection from?

RUIZ: Maybe you need it from me. What do you think? (*Reaches for gun.*)

(JENKIN *appears from the shadows.*)

JENKIN: Good evening, Señor Ruiz. (*Pause.*) You look as if you've had a hard day.

(RUIZ *is startled, looks confused.*)

Father Bravo and I are just about to drive to the Intercontinental for dinner.

RUIZ: Dinner?

JENKIN: With the British Ambassador. (RUIZ *grunts.*) Will you join us?

RUIZ: No, thank you. The American Ambassador tell me you go to see her too today. You mix in high places, Mr Jenkin. What did you talk about?

JENKIN: I had some new information about how Mary Tennant died.

RUIZ: From where did you get this? The government would like to know too.

JENKIN: From a young woman. She has made a statement.

RUIZ: What did this young woman say? You have a copy of the statement.

JENKIN: I'm a journalist, Señor Ruiz.

RUIZ: If you are a good journalist you know better than to believe what a young woman invents because she is angry and hurt.

JENKIN: I don't feel that's true in this case. (*To* RIGOBERTO) Listen, I do think it's time for us to go, we'll be late. (*To* RUIZ) Are you sure you won't join us?

RUIZ: No thank you. I came for confession. I didn't realize the father is busy. (*Moves towards the door.*) Is that your car at the bottom of the hill, Mr Jenkin? The blue Honda?

JENKIN: I don't know what sort of car it is. It's blue, yes.

RUIZ: The back door was not locked. Goodnight, my friends.
   (RUIZ *goes.* RIGOBERTO *beyond fury.*)

RIGOBERTO: *You crazy motherfucker! Why did you tell him it was your car?*
   (JENKIN *looks at the ceiling, expecting some response from above.*)
   You have put yourself in mortal danger with what you just tell him about Mrs Tennant.

JENKIN: I've been in mortal danger since I set foot in this place. I came out from under the altar in what I now think was a misguided attempt to intervene and save you from being shot to pieces.

RIGOBERTO: Thank you. So now we can't use your car.

JENKIN: I had no idea you were planning to use my car. Thank you for telling me. What the fuck is going on?

RIGOBERTO: Before that car goes a kilometre it will be drilled through like a coffee strainer. Ruiz does not do his dirty work and if he wants to kill you he will get men who do not know what you look like. They go by cars, you see. Blue Honda!
   (GRACE *comes in. She has an oily rag, is cleaning grease from her hands.* JENKIN *sits, shakes his head slowly.*)

57

Did you have luck?

GRACE: (*In Spanish*) No. There's a crack in the sump. Have you told him? We ought to leave now.

RIGOBERTO: He understands Spanish. The Honda is no use. I'm afraid Mr Jenkin has just made himself a potential martyr of the revolution by accusing Ruiz of a killing he did not commit. It is not safe to use the car tonight.

GRACE: We have to get away tonight, she needs treatment.
(JENKIN *raises his hands, lets them fall.* FOSTER *comes on behind.*)

RIGOBERTO: Your friend is in hiding in the *barrio*. We have to get her over the border into Nicaragua tonight. Our car is out of action.
(JENKIN *still.*)

FOSTER: This place is harder to get into than a Tibetan monastery. (*To* GRACE) I thought you'd be here.
(*They ignore him.* JENKIN *stands.*)

JENKIN: Can I see her?

FOSTER: I've always felt at home in Catholic churches. Perhaps I'm going to be a convert in my old age. Why is there is nearly half a ton of medical supplies in the crypt?

GRACE: To stop them being stolen. (*To* FOSTER) You see now why I couldn't tell you the truth.

FOSTER: I think Mrs Tennant had better talk to me. I shall wait a decent length of time so that you can get away before I do anything. (*To* JENKIN) I just want a short interview. (*Holds up pocket recorder.*) Otherwise as they say I may have to pull the plug.

RIGOBERTO: I'm not very frightened of you pulling plug, Mr Foster. We are already three-quarters of way down pipe.

FOSTER: I understand. I don't want to put you in any further danger.

JENKIN: How did you know about this?

FOSTER: I managed to get access to some intelligence information.

JENKIN: You were fed it by the Americans.

FOSTER: No, by our own people. They share information. What they didn't know was that Mrs Tennant was alive. She was

a bit of an embarrassment. They rather hoped she'd
disappear for good.

RIGOBERTO: Then we will make them happy. You have a car?

FOSTER: Yes. The Embassy lent me one.

RIGOBERTO: Good. That will be safe for us. If you let us have
your car I will let you have ten minutes with Mrs Tennant.

GRACE: No! Why should we? No . . .

RIGOBERTO: Fair deal.

FOSTER: How am I supposed to get back to town?

GRACE: You'll have to walk.

FOSTER: That's no good. Takes too long.

RIGOBERTO: Time is urgent to you? How long will it take you?
Two hour walk, three?

(FOSTER *pauses.*)

No car. No interview.

FOSTER: All right.

(FOSTER *takes out the keys, bounces them up and down in his
hand*.)

JENKIN: (*Standing*) I would like to see her. For a moment.

FOSTER: No, really, Bill, I'm sorry.

JENKIN: I have no intention of writing anything. I promise you.
I came here to see Mary. That is the truth!

RIGOBERTO: This is a moral question and a question of trust.
Mr Jenkin must see his friend. When you have finished
your business.

FOSTER: It's a question of trust. I don't trust him. (*Pockets the
keys*.) You need the car as much as I need to see Mrs
Tennant.

RIGOBERTO: OK. (*To* JENKIN) I'm sorry. (*To* FOSTER) I will
stay here with Mr Jenkin.

(FOSTER *separates a key from the ring*.)

FOSTER: That's the door key. I'll keep the ignition.

(*A pause*.)

I know this makes me seem like a complete shit.

GRACE: I've no idea, does it? I don't know what you want or
why. I never have done. There is no truth except the
innocent suffer most. If you stay here long enough you'll
have blood splashes on your shirt too. And if you're lucky it

59

will be somebody else's blood. All I can think about at the
moment is that I have to get a very badly injured woman to
a safe place where she can be treated.

(*She moves to go.*)

FOSTER: (*To* JENKIN) Is there anything you want to say? Any
message?

JENKIN: No, no . . . nothing. Give her my kind regards. Or
something like that.

(FOSTER *still for a moment. Then goes off after* GRACE.)

RIGOBERTO: I'm sorry you know now why I tell you lies. Ruiz
sent two men but they were drunk or drugged. She said
they could hardly stand up. They told her there was a baby
who was sick. Maybe the gun jammed. They had gone
when I got there. I can tell you she looked pretty dead.
Ruiz thinks she is dead. The Americans think too. And
your people. Everybody is trying to sweep the shit under
the rug. But the rug is still kicking.

(JENKIN *chuckles.*)

You have admiration for him.

JENKIN: Oh, absolutely, I'm afraid. Where do you think he
learned it? (*Pause.*) He will want to get a telex back as soon
as he gets to the hotel.

RIGOBERTO: The telexes are not very private here. Still we must
have the car.

(*He laughs.*)

JENKIN: I don't see why it's funny.

RIGOBERTO: Because he never thought to ask whether you have
car. And it is an obvious solution to our problems. You let
him have your car. You say you want to walk. He will be so
glad to get a quick trip to the hotel he won't think why you
are doing it.

(*A pause.*)

JENKIN: This could be loosely described as homicide.

RIGOBERTO: Who by? Not by me. Not by you.

JENKIN: No. I absolutely can't. No.

RIGOBERTO: We must have four hours from when we leave.

JENKIN: (*Holding up the newspaper*) The Bishop says you are a
well-known admirer of Che Guevara.

60

RIGOBERTO: I admire anyone who is capable of giving his life for a cause.

JENKIN: In this case, guerrilla warfare.

RIGOBERTO: I am not personally in favour of violence. But you yourself have graphic demonstration of the violence that is done to others.

(JENKIN *shakes his head slowly*.)

(*Angry*) We are doing this to survive!

JENKIN: I'm sorry, I can't let him take the car.

RIGOBERTO: We are slightly altering the laws of chance. You are increasing the chances of survival of three people one of whom is dear to you. And you must remember that your intervention, your meddling, has increased the danger for us. You can go home and write something very understanding. Maybe I if I am alive I will read it and say yes this is good, I recognize. But the world will have moved. Now you are in the middle and it is moving under your feet. And to be honest with you I would like to be remembered by you but not as a good story after dinner. And if you don't help it will be a sick story you will not want to tell anywhere.

JENKIN: I've spent half my life listening to moral blackmail and my response has always been the same. I'm far too old to change now.

RIGOBERTO: Perhaps they will not shoot up the car.

JENKIN: I'd rather take it myself. Do you understand?

(*Pause*.)

RIGOBERTO: So . . . We will bring him back here. Do your best to keep him here for as long as you can.

(JENKIN *lies down on the bench. Fiddles in his pocket*.)

I will leave you.

JENKIN: I'm pleased to have met you. I'm sorry, I'm rather tired . . . Would you give her this?

(*He hands* RIGOBERTO *the spider*. RIGOBERTO *studies it for a moment. He goes*. JENKIN *settles down to rest. Music. The lights dim*.)

Then come up. RIGOBERTO *is standing with* FOSTER *upstage*.
JENKIN *stirs slowly, wakes*.

RIGOBERTO: Mr Foster was surprised to learn you had a car.
(FOSTER *sits, very tense.*)
I will leave you. We have got, as they say, to ship our arses.
You have observed, Mr Jenkin. But you have done *nothing.*
Remember, Mr Jenkin, I am a pacifist. Jesus Christ is the
liberator. *Hasta pronto!*
(*He goes.* FOSTER *rubs his face with his hands.*)

JENKIN: You look terrible.

FOSTER: Look, I can't think of any reason why you should give
me a lift, but . . .

JENKIN: I would, Seb, only the bloody thing won't start. I tried
it half an hour ago.

FOSTER: Can we try it again? It's only eight. If I could get a
telex through in a couple of hours I could make the late
edition. Look, everything I told you about an invasion of
Nicaragua is true. Only there's no time to write a bloody
book about it.

JENKIN: I don't feel like moving at the moment. Like to talk to
you. I'm not feeling too good.

FOSTER: Let's give it a try. We can talk in the car.

JENKIN: I don't think I should move at the moment. I've got a
bit of a pain in my chest. I'm sure it's nothing serious.

FOSTER: It's important that I try to get through.

JENKIN: Give me five minutes. (*Pause.*) How is she? That's all I
want to know.

FOSTER: She's still in a lot of pain. She didn't say very much.

JENKIN: God, I could do with a drink. There wasn't a message
or anything like that, was there?

FOSTER: Oh. (*Pats his shirt pocket.*) I nearly forgot. (*Produces an
envelope.*) She gave me this.
(JENKIN *takes it, glances at it briefly. Puts it away. Stares at*
FOSTER.)
Are you all right?

JENKIN: Just *déjà vu* . . . Falklands. The lost copy.

FOSTER: There was a lot of petty jealousy. It may have
happened once. In the heat of it all. I can't remember. You
know what it's like. For Christ's sake I thought that was all
dead and buried. I didn't think you listened to gossip.

JENKIN: I heard it happened more than once, Seb.

FOSTER: You are a fucking hypocrite, Bill. You once boasted to me that you paid twelve Vietnamese peasants a day's wages to pig the telephone lines in the Saigon Hilton to stop anyone else getting a story through.

JENKIN: *Touché*. But there was a small necessity beyond my own joy, which I freely admit, in putting one over on my colleagues. If you come face to face with the truth it's really very satisfying to stuff the ones who couldn't care less. As it happened I'd spent two weeks going to endless press briefings listening to the Americans telling me lies about how they were winning the war against the Viet Cong. As soon as I saw what was really happening it seemed the only imaginative thing to do. All you were writing from the South Atlantic was a lot of stirringly written jingoism you knew most people at home wanted to hear and which bought you preferential treatment by the army. And helped you to write a bestselling book.

FOSTER: Bill, there was nothing to be said for the Argentinians. You said that yourself. From the comfort of your armchair.

JENKIN: Wasn't there a lot to be said about the mess and the chaos? When the true story came back it was too late to influence anything. And the truth is it would have been too unpopular, wouldn't it? And yet there were people who were prepared to say unpopular things, I think, weren't there?

FOSTER: I wrote what I felt at the time. You taught me that. For God's sake, Bill!

JENKIN: Of course.

FOSTER: We have to be there first. We have to be better informed. And we have to tell both sides of the story . . . objectively.

(*A pause.* JENKIN *looks at the note.*)

JENKIN: You opened the envelope. (*Slight pause.*) I hope you were suitably embarrassed.

(FOSTER *uneasy.*)

FOSTER: How are you feeling?

JENKIN: Very unlike moving.

(*Pause.*)

FOSTER: I don't want us to fall out about this. It's the last thing in the world I want.

JENKIN: What are you going to write?

FOSTER: I can't tell you, Bill.

JENKIN: Give them a few hours to get to the border. They're decent people.

FOSTER: Mrs Tennant gives information to the Sandinistas in Nicaragua about troop movements this side of the border. Because she's a Christian Aid worker she's been able to move around without anybody suspecting her. Until recently.

JENKIN: I know. (*Pause.*) If you send a telex to your paper from the Intercontinental, the army, the police, the entire staff of the American Embassy not to mention the British Embassy will have it in five minutes. Let's forget the car and wander into town together. It's a beautiful night. I'll be fine in half an hour.

FOSTER: They've taken full responsibility for what they're doing. (*Moves over to* JENKIN.) I really have to have those keys, Bill.

JENKIN: I'm not ready to move.

FOSTER: I don't want to take them from you, because you're not well, Bill. But I will if I have to.

JENKIN: I think you should give them time to reach the border.

FOSTER: (*Quietly*) Let me have the keys.
   (JENKIN *half stands, sits down again.*)
   Are you all right? (*Pause.*) Bill . . .

JENKIN: I taught you . . . if I taught you anything. I taught you . . . (*suddenly angry*) about *gut* feelings. Compassion. Where did I go wrong?

FOSTER: Haven't you noticed how fast information travels these days? We only have a few seconds to scratch a message on the retina. (*Grins.*) I am Apollo's little sidekick! I am the telex made flesh and I am a fucking reporter not a philosopher. Are you going to give me the keys?

JENKIN: (*He jingles them in his pocket*) You'll have to make a pass at me or beat me unconscious to get them. Do you understand? Three people are going to die unless you wait until tomorrow.

FOSTER: Tomorrow. I can't even wait an hour.

JENKIN: Three decent people.

FOSTER: I'd like to agree with you. But I don't trust anyone's motives. The world's a heap of shit.

JENKIN: Get out of the job.

FOSTER: I like the game, Bill. I don't need to feel superior. Keys.

JENKIN: You'll have to knock me out. I told you.

FOSTER: For Christ's sake . . .

JENKIN: I mean it . . .

FOSTER: I don't have time!

JENKIN: I mean it!

FOSTER: (*Advancing*) All right, Bill . . .

JENKIN: (*Holds up a hand*) All right.

(JENKIN *takes out the car keys. Tosses them so they fall on the floor. A pause.*)

FOSTER: You want me to grovel for them. I don't blame you.

(*Picks them up.* JENKIN *impassive, silent.*)

Thank you. Whatever you say, I still respect you more than anyone, Bill. (*Angrily*) You were never so fucking moral.

JENKIN: You can't have been listening.

FOSTER: Hasta luego.

JENKIN: I don't think there's much wrong with the car. I probably flooded it.

FOSTER: I'll see you in the bar at the Intercontinental.

(JENKIN *doesn't react.*)

There'll be a large whisky waiting for you.

(FOSTER *goes.* JENKIN *still. The* TWO INDIANS, *still in clay masks, come in. They are drunk, giggling. They are carrying the Virgin.* JENKIN *still, they don't appear to notice him. They put the Virgin down, and go out.* JENKIN *gets up, goes stumbling upstage. He stops, comes down again. Seems to be about to kneel. Gets down on one knee. Pause. Gets up again. Sound of a car, then another car. Stands looking at the Virgin. A skid. Sound of a machine-gun. Lights fade.*)

Then up again, JENKIN *in spot, as before. His ear has a cleaner, smaller bandage. He has a clean shirt on.*

65

JENKIN: The old woman said that when the men crossed the street, the children ran away. And the Englishwoman disappeared . . . and being one of a particular breed, she turned up somewhere else. We have always taken this kind of woman to our hearts; a much travelled woman, an eccentric, wilful and determined, the kind of woman who inspires endless anecdotes and mountains of literature. They're often reviled in their lifetime, their enemies may far outnumber their friends. It may be that we British prefer our heroines dead. But anyway, a fitting subject for a final column. (*The hint of a pause.*) I've spent the whole of this afternoon in a bar in Managua, the capital of Nicaragua, which you may or may not know had a revolution a few years ago. I've been drinking far too much *cerveza Victoria* with the kind of people I like; a Catholic priest who is also a poet, a beautiful Canadian woman who has seemingly dedicated her life to stitching up the mess that the world leaves in its wake . . . and this remarkable Englishwoman. We are waiting for an invasion that has not yet happened, which for different reasons we hope will not happen. Quite naturally the talk has been of America and Americans. At many turning points in my life it has been the same thing. It was obvious that all of us, despite our wildly different ages and our disparate backgrounds, shared a common respect for the founding ideals of the nation that for better or worse seems to control our lives. (*Wipes his forehead with a handkerchief.*) When I walked round this gaunt, earthquake-ruined city this Sunday morning and watched the thousands going to church, it was difficult for a few moments to believe that this was a revolutionary country, albeit one with three Catholic priests in the government. But the commonest slogan on the walls is *Todas las Armas al Pueblo* – 'Give all the Arms to the People', which when I thought about it was a very odd slogan indeed for a revolutionary country, unless you are thinking of revolutions in terms of the American revolution and not the ones in the East. I've visited quite a number of totalitarian countries of both the Right and the Left and

66

there is one thing they have in common. A very great reluctance to *Todas las Armas al Pueblo*. The Englishwoman, who has seen more of the world than I have and I have no reason to doubt her, said there was only one other country in the world with the confidence in its own people to allow everyone the right to own a gun. Coming from a Central American country where the guns are in the hands of a minority and are mostly trained unerringly on its own people, it seems a luxury to make my ending such a paradox, an irony and if I seem partial or biased, you must, as ever . . . forgive me.

(*The lights fade on* JENKIN.)

Light grows again, dimly. The MOTHERS OF THE DISAPPEARED, *led by* NORA, *come on. They are disguised in dark glasses, dark clothes and shawls. Their white banners and placards fill the stage. On the placards are pasted photographs of missing people. The dates of their disappearance. Their ages, their jobs. As the lights dim again, music comes up again quite loud. From* Guittara Armada, A Gaspar.

67